PLANNING PAYS OFF

I0589332

PLANNING PAYS OFF
by Jerry D. Young
Published by Creative Texts Publishers, LLC

Copyright 2015-2017 by Jerry D. Young
All rights reserved
Cover photo modified and used by license.
Credit: The U.S. Army

This book or parts thereof may not be reproduced in any form, stored in a retrieval system, or transmitted in any form by any means—electronic, mechanical, photocopy, recording, or otherwise—without prior written permission of the publisher, except as provided by United States of America copyright law.

The following is a work of fiction. Any resemblance to actual names, persons, businesses, and incidents is strictly coincidental. Locations are used only in the general sense and do not represent the real place in actuality.

ISBN: 978-0-692-50951-7

PLANNING PAYS OFF

by

JERRY D. YOUNG

CHAPTER ONE

-

Sven Denali jerked awake when the Oregon Scientific weather radio alarm went off. He fumbled on the bedside lamp and picked up the radio, trying to read the warning as his eyes adjusted to the light. He didn't have to read it on the display. The announcer started speaking. Sven noticed the difference in tone from the usual broadcasts of tornadoes and blizzards.

His voice was actually shaking.

"This is an announcement from the President of the United States of America"

Sven swung his legs around and put his feet on the floor, fully awake now.

"My fellow Americans", came the president's voice from the speaker. "Now is the time for all of us to pull together. We expect…"

The president's words stopped and the weather radio squealed for a moment and then fell silent. At the same time, bright light flooded the bedroom from outside.

"Uh-oh!" Sven said under his breath and dove for the floor beside the bed, wrapping his arms around his head to protect it. Most of the glass from the windows when they shattered landed on the bed and floor, only a little landed on his bare back. The reverse wave whistled and Sven knew windows on the other side of the house were now in shards, too.

Sven waited for a little while longer and the ground shock shook the house. He heard something crash somewhere, but couldn't tell what it was. An interminable two minutes later, clad only in the boxer shorts he wore to bed, Sven slipped his feet into the sandals he kept by the bed. After shaking them clear of glass, he grabbed the Colt 1911A1 .45 pistol and the Maglite six D-cell flashlight from the bedside table and headed for the basement of the house.

There was still some light coming through the ripped shades of the windows, but it was an eerie purplish and orange color. He turned on the bright flashlight and kept going. There was glass everywhere, as well as debris from the shaking the house had suffered from the blast waves.

The stairs to the basement were intact, though Sven had to put his weight against the upper part of the door to get it open to have access to them. Sven was now a bit concerned the hatch to his fallout shelter might be difficult to open also. Sven moved the cabinet hiding it from view, worked the combination of the safe door, and spun the opening handle.

Sven let out a sigh of relief as the heavy, counter-balanced door swung open easily at Sven's steady push. Another couple of moments and Sven was inside the shelter, closing the door behind him. A flip of a switch and the shelter lights came on and he turned off the Maglite flashlight.

It took a few moments to calibrate a pen-style radiation dosimeter and clip it to the Tyvek suit with a hood he put on. He added rubber boots, a respirator, and rubber gloves before opening the access door and going back into the basement, Colt and Maglite again in hand.

Instead of moving to the stairs of the basement, Sven moved to the out-door entrance of the basement and opened it slowly and carefully. There was something lying on it, but he was able to push the slanted doors open and step out. It was a piece of his neighbor's roof that had partially blocked the door.

Sven left the Maglite turned off as he walked around his house. There was enough of the purplish/orange light to be able to tell the house wasn't going to be repairable. Not if what he thought was happening was really happening. The still forming mushroom cloud off to the east sure was a good indication that it was—a nuclear attack on the US. The President was in the act of warning the population about it when it happened.

Sven turned off all the utilities where each one entered the house. Hearing cursing

3

from someone nearby, Sven weighed the pros and cons of contacting the neighbors. He'd long ago made the decision to isolate himself and let everyone else cope the best they knew how in the event of a major disaster, but now he hesitated.

What if…

The gunshots in the near distance decided him. "Follow the plan," he voiced, and then turned and hurried back to the outside basement entrance. He realized he should have acted faster when his neighbor, Zander Smith, called over.

"Is that you over there, Sven?"

A feeble beam of light accompanied the voice. It barely reached Sven, but there was enough light for Zander and his wife to see the white Tyvek suit, respirator, and Maglite. Sven was holding the Colt slightly behind his hip and out mostly of sight.

Glenda, Zander's wife, screamed loudly when she saw Sven.

"You better get out of here, whoever you are," Zander said, taking Glenda into one arm. "Sven won't like it, you messing with his stuff."

"It's me, Zander!" Sven said. There wasn't anything coming from the sky at the moment so he lifted the respirator so the two could see his face.

"Sven? What are you doing? Why are you wearing that? And is that a gun?"

"No. Flashlight," Sven said, turning the bright beam on. "This is the gun," he added, holding it up.

Zander and Glenda shrank back from him.

"I suggest the two of you get in your basement and try to rig up some fallout protection," Sven said and turned around to go down into the basement.

"What about you?" Zander asked. "Could you show us?"

Sven could have kicked himself. It just slipped out. "I've got shelter. There isn't enough time…"

"You have a shelter?" Zander asked, the two now moving slowly toward him.

"For me," Sven said. "You need to back up". He was watching the two continue to advance towards him.

"You have to let us in, man!" cried Zander. "If you have a shelter…it's the only thing to do. Come on Glenda!"

Zander took a much larger step forward.

Sven lifted the Colt. "I'm sorry, Zander" he said. "It's a very small shelter and there isn't enough room or food for all of us."

"You can't do that!" Glenda was screaming and she pulled free from Zander, taking several more steps forward. "Take me in! I'll do anything you want! There is enough for two, isn't there?"

"Glenda!" exclaimed Zander.

Before Sven could react, Zander was lifting the little pistol he had been clutching in his free hand in his pocket. Sven began to lift the Colt, but Zander didn't shoot at him. Instead, he shot his wife in the back, the gun making very little noise.

"Crimeny!" Sven yelled, now with his gun pointed at Zander.

"Just two, right? Zander said, taking yet another step further. "You and me. We're buddies. You'll take me in, won't you?"

"Not just no, but…" Sven didn't finish the comment. Zander was shooting at him this time. Sven dived for the open basement doors and rolled down the steps after snapping off a quick shot at Zander.

Climbing to his feet, Sven ran to the shelter entrance, went through, and heaved it closed. He yelped in pain when he put his shoulder against it to move it faster. A bullet hit the door and whined off somewhere in the shelter, but the door was closed and Sven spun the locking handle before Zander could get to it.

Sven reached over his right shoulder with his left hand after setting the Maglite down. The hand came away bloody.

"That SOB shot me!"

Sven leaned back against the shelter door and then slid down to a seated position, losing consciousness as he did so.

It wasn't until he looked at his watch when he came to that Sven realized he'd been out for over an hour. He groaned when he tried to use his right hand and arm to push himself up. He quit doing that and rolled over to his left, finally managing to get up.

There was total silence in the shelter, except for his breathing. Concerned about his shoulder, Sven stripped again, taking enough time to look through the dosimeter. It was still on zero. There'd been no fallout while he was outside.

After a shower, Sven tried to get a look at the shoulder. Eventually, he used a hand-held mirror, along with the mirror in the tiny bathroom of the shelter, and got a look. There was a tiny puckered hole over the shoulder blade on his right side. There was a tiny spot of blood in the center of it. Despite an extensive first-aid kit, all Sven could do was apply a dab of triple antibiotic ointment on it and cover it with a simple Band-Aid.

He moved his shoulder around. There was no restriction of movement, but the muscles were stiff. Sven wondered what was going on. He had a cheap AM/FM radio and connected it to an outside wire antenna, after

7

un-grounding the wire. Only static could be heard on both bands. Disconnecting the antenna and grounding it once more, Sven went over to the door of the shelter and put his ear against it. He couldn't hear anything, though there was an occasional vibration that Sven put off to distant nuclear detonation ground waves.

With nothing better to do, Sven went to one of the two bunks in the shelter, crawled into the lower one, rolled over, and went to sleep.

Glancing at his watch when he woke up, Sven noted the time. He'd either slept four hours and it was seven in the morning, or sixteen hours and it was seven in the evening of the day after the attack started. The way his bladder was feeling, Sven figured he'd been asleep the sixteen hours.

After going to the bathroom, despite his growling stomach—another indication it had been sixteen hours—Sven hooked up the little AM/FM radio.

Static again. Possibly slightly less than before.

Turning to the CD V-717 remote reading survey meter, Sven checked for fallout. He smiled, only about twelve Röentgens per hour. Unless he got some from targets to his west, he should be able to leave the shelter in a few days. Satisfied there was nothing more to do, Sven prepared a meal, picked one of the paperback westerns he had stored in the shelter, and began to read.

That's what he did for two weeks. Eat, sleep, read, and check the radio and radiation meter. There must have been some additional fallout from somewhere, for the level didn't fall quite as quickly as Sven expected. He decided to just stay an entire two weeks, just because. It was better to be safe than sorry, anyway, and he had plenty of westerns.

When he suited up again, in a Tyvek suit without a bullet hole, the radiation was under 0.05 R/hr. Nothing to worry about, as long as he was careful not to inhale any of the fallout, or carry it back into the shelter with him after being outside.

After pressing his ear against the shelter door and hearing nothing, Sven fastened the respirator into place and tried to spin the opener wheel. It moved a partial turn and stopped. Despite his best efforts, Sven couldn't get the locking mechanism to unlock.

"Well, nuts!" Sven said. He walked across the shelter and crawled into the open end of a thirty-inch culvert. Wishing he had kneepads on, he made his way the full length of the culvert. Sven situated himself at the end of the culvert so he could release the doors above the pit that ended the culvert.

When he released the doors, sand began to fall into the pit. It took less than a minute and the sand quit falling. Shining the bright Maglite up to the bottom side of a sagging layer of grass, Sven got into the pit, pulled the Colt from his pocket, and stood up, pushing through the grass mat aside without any problems.

He did a quick full three-sixty to get a look around for possible trouble. Seeing nothing but damaged houses, his included, Sven climbed up out of the hole and got to his feet. Moving cautiously, he checked the houses closest to his for any sign of anyone. He found no one living. Whoever had gone through the houses scavenging for food didn't seem to be around. There were plenty of dead bodies, however, both inside and outside, including Glenda's.

Having seen plenty of death while in the service, he didn't think too much about it until he realized that Glenda's body wasn't where it had fallen when Zander shot her. There were some signs of depredation, but not from something that could have moved the body. Sven then realized that she hadn't died instantly.

Shaking his head, Sven looked over at the yard shed. It had collapsed into itself. Deciding to worry about it later, Sven went to the front door of his house. It hung loose. It had been closed and locked when Sven had gone to bed that fateful night. The scavengers had been in his house, too.

As he had the other houses, Sven went through his own with the pistol up and ready. Also like the others, the fridge and pantry shelves had been cleaned out of everything edible at some point between the attack and now.

More curious now than worried about why the main door of the shelter wouldn't open, Sven went down stairs to take a look there. That's when he gagged and almost threw up in the respirator.

Zander was there, plus a couple more of the neighbors.

Dead.

They had all died badly, judging from the amount of blood showing on the walls, floor, and even the ceiling of the basement. Not to mention the equally bloody axe, pick-mattock, and sledge hammer that were all laying nearby. Then Sven noticed the empty cartridge cases at the foot of the stairs.

The best explanation he could come up with was that Zander, probably alone initially, had tried to break into the shelter door. That was why it wouldn't open. The locking mechanism had kept the vault locked under the assault of the sledge hammer, pick-mattock, axe, and bullets, but now it couldn't be opened due to the damage.

At some point, some of the neighbors must have tried to take over or just help. Something went wrong, probably panic, and they set on one another. Perhaps it was triggered by the scavengers. Perhaps they came later. Sven couldn't tell and didn't want to hang around the mess to try to figure it out. Seven people were dead at the entrance to his shelter, some having died horrible deaths.

When Sven turned to leave the basement, something caught his eye near where the remains of Zander's body lay. It was the tiny pistol he'd used. A Raven .25 ACP. That explained the fact that Sven wasn't injured worse than he had been when shot with the diminutive round, though it had served its purpose with Glenda, even if she didn't die immediately.

Sven started to leave it where it lay, but turned around and picked it up. Never knew when another gun might come in handy, even a Raven .25.

Next on the agenda was to check on the truck in the garage. The truck seemed to be just fine, but Sven couldn't get the garage door open. Leaving it for the moment, Sven went back into the shelter the way he'd come out, through the escape tunnel.

He didn't bother to decontaminate, going straight in. With the respirator tilted back on the top of his head, Sven went through the small shelter and moved everything he was going to keep, slowly and painfully, through the tunnel. He piled it all outside, near the tunnel exit. Some things were a tight fit and difficult to handle going through the tunnel, but Sven kept at it and finally had what he wanted sitting beside the tunnel opening.

He did the same with things in the rest of the house, though there weren't that many things he wanted from inside. The task done, Sven rested a while. When he got up out of the folding chair, he moved once again to the garage. He tried a couple of other options to get the garage door open, but the frame was just too warped for the door to move.

"Well, nuts!" Sven exclaimed. He then went about loading a few things from the shelves in the garage into the back of his old Suburban in the dim light coming through the two windows in the garage. Then he lowered the two preloaded Thule cargo containers onto the roof rack of the Suburban and fastened them in place.

Next, Sven put the hitch mount cargo box in place and loaded it up with the last of the things he wanted from the garage. He hesitated then, but finally went back into the house and into the basement. There were a few things he wanted from there. He just hated to be around the gore.

After three trips he had everything, including the bloody tools. Those he placed in the roof cargo rack between the two Thule units. The other things went into the back of the Suburban, through the right side passenger door.

Knowing he couldn't put it off any longer, Sven got behind the wheel of the Suburban, crossed his fingers for a moment, and then turned the key to start it. He grinned when the diesel fired right up. It was a non-electronic diesel and he hadn't been too worried about EMP, but it was good to know the engine would run.

Leaving the engine running, Sven got out, dug out a pair of large bolt cutters from the rear box and climbed up onto the bumper and grill guard on the front of the Suburban. It took only a couple of moments to cut the cable of the electric door opener, and then the two cables that connected to the counter-balance springs.

There was a terrible racket as the springs unwound and the door fell downward, only two inches, still in its tracks. After putting the bolt cutter away, Sven got back into the driver's seat of the Suburban.

Putting the transmission in low, Sven eased the Suburban forward until the heavy bumper and brush guard was against the door. Giving the diesel just a bit more throttle, Sven began to push against the door. It was no match for the Suburban and began to crack and splinter as Sven kept going.

A bit further and the rollers jumped out of the tracks and the garage door fell, the upper panels slamming onto the hood and then sliding off. Sven winced. "There goes the paint!" he muttered. But he didn't stop. He rolled right over the remains of the door onto the parking pad.

A few minutes later and he was backed up to the similar garage door in the yard shed. There was no way he could just cut the door loose the way he had the one in the garage, things were just too jumbled up.

"Oh, well, I built the trailer to take it…" he said aloud and got into the rear cargo box again. Taking out a hitch mount winch, he slid it into place in the extension tube of the hitch on the cargo box and locked it into place.

With a grimace, Sven climbed up the access ladder on the rear of the Suburban and retrieved the bloody axe. At least he had his gloves on. It took only a few swings with the axe to make a hole in the door at one side so he could run the winch cable through, pull it around and snap the hook into the tow hook on the rear bumper.

He'd put the Suburban in four-wheel drive when he was moving it, in anticipation of what he was ready to do. He eased the Suburban forward, felt the cable tension, and then pressed the accelerator a bit more. The Suburban sort of grunted, but eased forward amidst the screeching noises of the yard shed coming apart at the seams.

Then the Suburban surged forward and Sven brought it to a stop. He got out to look at the result. Sure enough, the garage door and frame had finally pulled loose. But the shed had collapsed the rest of the way down onto the custom trailer that was inside.

Sven dragged the door out of the way, unhooked the winch and put it away, and inserted a pintle hitch into the hitch tube, locking it securely into place. He backed the Suburban up to the tandem wheeled trailer. There was just enough clearance for him to make contact with the trailer. He set the brake, hopped out, and connected the hitch ring of the trailer to the pintle hitch on the Suburban. He plugged up the wiring connection, and the fuel line from the tanks in the trailer, and then got back into the Suburban.

When he pulled forward the trailer eased out of the collapsing shed easily and Sven sighed with relief. The trailer wasn't an absolute necessity, but he really wanted it with him on his upcoming journey.

Working very carefully, Sven loaded a few things from the remains of the shed onto the trailer, careful not to let the structure collapse on him. He finally looked around one last time, stripped off the protective equipment, shaking it off and putting it in the Suburban, and started to get behind the driver's seat again.

The voice came out of the blue. "Put your hands up and step away from the rig, dude, and I won't kill you."

Sven did as requested, turning slightly so he could see who was talking. There were two of them. Both in their twenties, Sven thought, and both armed, one with a twenty-two-caliber revolver, and the other a very dangerous looking semi-automatic. Sven was pretty sure it was a Hi-Point, but he wasn't sure. It didn't really make any difference; a 9mm bullet from it was just as dangerous as one from a Browning Hi-Power.

"You don't need to do this," Sven said slowly. He noted both men's appearance. Both were suffering from radiation sickness, and probably malnutrition. "I'm willing to help…"

"Shut up!" screamed the man with the .22 revolver, waving the gun menacingly toward Sven.

The other said, "Let's just kill him and take his stuff." He held the pistol loosely in his hand, in the classic on-the-side gangsta hold.

Sven had the sudden feeling that was just what the two were going to do. He had nothing else to lose. Sven dived to the men's left, hitting the ground rolling, grabbing for the Colt in the small of the back holster.

Several shots rang out and Sven had to think for a moment to figure out if he'd been hit or not. It didn't seem so, and both of the men were down. Still trying to sense if he'd been shot, Sven got up and walked carefully over to the two men. Revolver man was dead where he lay.

Sven kicked the gun out of his reach anyway, his eyes turning to the pistol packer. He wasn't dead, but if Sven was any judge, and he was, it wouldn't be long. Unless Sven put him out of his misery, it would be a painful death. Two of Sven's rounds had hit him in the stomach, another in the thigh, which was what took him down.

Again, Sven slid the gun away from possible access and then bent down to pick it up. It was indeed a Hi-Point 9mm. When Sven leaned down and began to go through the man's pockets he screamed in pain. But Sven found three more magazines for the pistol, a partial box of ammunition, and no less than three knives.

As the glazed eyes of the moaning man looked on, Sven searched the other guy. He found two fifty-round boxes of .22's, and only two knives, but the revolver was a Ruger Single Six, and, like the other man's, the knives were Cold Steel and Spyderco brands. "Wonder if they got a package deal?" went through Sven's mind as he gathered everything up.

"What about me, mister?" groaned the wounded man.

"It's simple, dude. You lost. You die. Now, if you want, I can put a bullet in the back of your head, or you can just lay there and die."

There was enough attitude in him for the man to reply with a string of expletives. Sven got into the Suburban and drove away. He almost turned back when he saw the pack of dogs roaming near the entrance to his subdivision. They were a sorry looking bunch of dogs, and probably didn't have long to live themselves. But, if they picked up the smell of blood, and Sven thought they looked like they had, the gangsta still alive would die even harder than the stomach wound would cause.

Putting it out of his mind, Sven kept going, heading for where he knew he should have been at the time of the attack.

CHAPTER TWO

-

Sven reached over and adjusted the rifle leaning against the passenger seat to an easier position for him to grab and use if he needed to do so. He'd been careless at the house and could have wound up with another bullet hole in him, or as dead as the gangstas, with his rig in their possession. It would be one thing to die and have a family get his stuff, but he wasn't about to let lowlifes get it and use it to terrorize even more people.

If he had been able to implement Plan A, nothing that had happened the last two weeks or so would have occurred the same way. He would have been where he was now heading. Hopefully he could make it to his small retreat on Lake Wappapello, north of Poplar Bluff, Missouri without any more encounters like the last one.

Nothing happened at first, but he did have to change the route. His keychain radiation alarm began to chirp. Sven turned the rig around and retraced the route until the alarm stopped sounding. Sven took out a map to check his alternate route.

The best alternate would take him back into the fallout zone for a bit, but would then turn away from it...probably. It depended on the actual fallout pattern and there was no way for Sven to determine that without going through it. The risk was too high. That meant an alternate to the alternate.

With the Yaesu FT-819D scanning the Amateur HF frequencies, Sven turned the Suburban south, rather than east. He hoped to be able to contact an Amateur with some information, as none of the broadcast stations seemed to be on the air. He'd had no contact, except the Gangstas, since the attack. All the radios had been silent except for static. He had tested his equipment and everything seemed to have survived in the faraday cages he'd stored it in.

Sven kept edging east, when a road was available, but he kept hitting the fallout line and had to keep going more southward. He was beginning to get a bit worried that the retreat site might have taken much more fallout than he had thought would be likely.

There had been no real certainties when he was looking for the property. It was a tossup whether the empty silos associated with Whiteman Air Force base would be hit. It was almost a certainty that Whiteman would be, but that would be only two or three small devices. If whoever it was hit the empty missile silos, there would be much more fallout going southeast from them, perhaps enough to keep the retreat off-limits for some time to come.

Sven put the possibilities out of his head and kept his attention on the road and his surroundings. If there were more bad guys, or even some good guys with too good of an opportunity, he could be attacked for his working vehicle.

He'd seen many others stranded on the road, though there had been only a couple of dead visible in one of them. Everyone had apparently sought shelter somewhere when their automobiles quit. Sven had no doubt it would have been much worse if the EMP had come during a morning or evening commute rather than so early in the morning.

Sven was getting hungry around five in the afternoon and began looking for a place to stop and eat, and perhaps lay over for the night. He was on a southeasterly course and the alarm began to sound again.

With a sigh, Sven turned around, intending to head back to the last place he could go more southward. Only a minute or so on the back trail and he saw two pickup trucks. For the first moments, he thought they were stopped on the road, but he suddenly realized that he hadn't seen them when he came past that point earlier.

Sven slowed down and came to a stop. The two pickups were slowly approaching. Whoever they were, they weren't very smart.

When they realized that the Suburban had come to a stop, several of the occupants in the beds of the pickups began firing. It settled one problem for Sven. He didn't have to wonder if they were friendly or not.

Stepping out of the Suburban, Sven brought the PTR-91 with him. He had a Beta-C dual drum magazine in it and began to empty it toward the two trucks as they accelerated toward him. He must have had a lucky shot for one of the trucks immediately slowed down and rolled off the road, nose down in the ditch. The other one kept coming.

Sven got back into the Suburban, started it forward just enough to let the four-wheel drive engage, and then turned off the pavement. It was a rough ride, but the Suburban and trailer both made the transition from pavement to dirt through the ditch without trouble. The other truck immediately tried the same thing, and made it across the ditch, though with two less people in the bed of the truck than were in there originally.

Keeping the speed up as much as he dared, and that was quite a bit, he was pulling away from the pickup when it slowed and stopped. Sven kept going, glancing in the rearview mirror from time to time.

The pursuing truck had turned around and was headed back toward the other. Fortunately, the best route out of the pending ambush was to the south, away from the fallout, and Sven kept going until he could pick up a road.

When he got back onto pavement he stopped and did a quick walk around of the vehicle. There didn't seem to be any damage until he got to the back of the trailer. There were a couple of bullet marks on the metal, but they'd been glancing blows along the side of the trailer and had only scratched the paint and dented the metal.

Sven hit the road again, looking for a likely place to stop, security the uppermost in his mind. He found a gravel road that led off the two lane highway fairly soon and turned off onto it. It went into a stand of trees and just sort of petered out. Sven managed to get the Suburban and trailer turned around in the tight space, and parked with the rig headed back the way they'd come into the trees.

Taking four of his passive infrared perimeter alarms from the Suburban, Sven set them around the camp area and turned them on. He went about setting up his tent and then prepared a quick meal, opening up an MRE and heating the entrée with the heater included in the package. He ate the side dishes and desert slowly after he ate the entrée, savoring every bite.

After going into the trees to dig a cat hole, just inside the range of the alarm system, he did his business. He covered the hole and went back to the tent. The twilight was now darkness and Sven didn't use a light when he rolled out the sleeping pad and then the bag. He stripped down and slid into the cotton liner already in the bag, setting the Colt within reach. The PTR was again loaded with a full drum. It was handy by the door of the tent. Sven closed his eyes and was soon asleep.

He slept well, though he did wake up a couple of times. There were no alarms, but Sven had the Colt in his hand when he left the tent to go to the bathroom and take a look around. Satisfied he was alone, Sven set about getting breakfast. It didn't take long. When he had eaten and broken camp, he fired the Suburban up and left less than forty-five minutes from the time he had left the tent.

He was even with Joplin, Missouri. Sven stopped and hesitated. It wasn't that far to Tulsa. He had family in Tulsa, but they should be either at the retreat or on their way, just like him.

He kept going, eastward again, feeling hopeful that the radiation alarm wouldn't start sounding. He was only a few miles south of where his retreat was on Wappapello Lake, more or less on a line with Poplar Bluff. He began to relax some when he picked up US 160 north of Branson. Though 160 would take him further south, Sven decided to stay on it unless there was an overwhelming reason to leave it. It meant he would have to cut north, either through Poplar Bluff, or take a route around it, to get to the retreat.

The look of the weather began to bother him. There'd been no immediate 'Nuclear Winter,' the way some scenarios had predicted, but it was suddenly uncommonly cold for this far south at this time of year. The sky had been hazy ever since Sven had left the shelter, but now real clouds were forming. It looked like it could be a really bad storm.

Trying to keep an eye on the storm that was building behind him, Sven almost didn't see the roadblock ahead in time. He was on the west side of the small town where the 160 crossed an arm of Bull Shoals Lake.

Sven checked the rear view mirror when he came to a stop. Sure enough, he'd missed the blocking force. "They must have been on one of the side roads," Sven muttered to himself. They were approaching slowly and Sven debated another minute to take a quick look at the map before he took his foot off the brake pedal and put it on the accelerator. He began moving forward again. He was in what was essentially a cul-de-sac. Any of the side roads would take him to a dead end or another roadblock, he was sure.

The blocking force stayed well behind when Sven stopped twenty-feet or so from the road block. He kept his hands up, in sight, after he opened the driver's side door of the Suburban, and got out very slowly.

"Just passing through!" he called out, facing the roadblock. He hadn't seen anyone, but felt like there were a dozen pairs of eyes on him. Finally, a man stepped from behind one of the cars that made up the roadblock. He had a shotgun, the butt resting on his hip.

"This is a toll road now," said the man. "Going either way. Once you passed through our line, you owed us."

"How much? Will you take a check?"

The man didn't like that, at all. The shotgun came down of his hip and was now held in two hands. "Not funny, guy. Not much humor left in the world. I'd be careful where you tried to dish it out. Now fork over five gallons of gas or we'll look things over and take what we want."

"How about diesel?" Sven asked.

"Diesel is fine."

"I'll get it out of the trailer," Sven said, and turned to go back to do it.

"Easy," said the man, walking forward now to join Sven. "Okay. Any funny moves and you're dead and we're rich, from the look of your rig."

Sven took the threat to heart. He lifted the lid of one of the side toolboxes of the trailer and pulled out a jerry can. He tried to hand it to the man, but the man backed up. "Set it down on the side of the road."

After doing so, the man waved toward the roadblock and one of the cars began to move, being pushed manually by two more people.

"In your rig and get out of here. I'd suggest you don't come back. Things are going to get tough and we have to take care of our families any way we can."

Sven simply nodded, got into the Suburban and pulled through the gap in the roadblock. There were some people about in the small town, but they simply stared at Sven driving by, making no move to wave or speak.

When he reached the other side of the town, he drove through the gap already opened in that roadblock. "After all that," Sven said aloud, "I hope the bridge is okay." It was and Sven crossed it, vowing to himself to be more careful. He wasn't sure if there had been anything he could have done. The roadblock had been placed well and the blocking force knew what they were doing.

Shaking off the almost doom-like feeling, Sven continued on his way at a slightly more sedate pace, watching carefully ahead. He did continue to take a glance in the rearview mirror, both to check on the approaching storm and to make sure he wasn't being followed.

The town on the other side of the lake seemed to be abandoned. He saw no one, not even a stray dog, as he passed through the town at a moderate speed. He sighed in relief when he cleared the town and was on the open road again.

Stopping well before getting to each of the small towns he came to he would study the map and find a way around them on county roads. He even used some farm roads. The process, while apparently safer, was much more time consuming.

The storm caught up with him just outside of West Plains. He decided to wait it out in the Suburban after finding a bare field adjacent to the highway where he could park. Sven turned off the engine of the Suburban and leaned the seat back to get comfortable, taking the Colt from the seat next to him to hold in his lap.

It was a fitful evening and night. The storm raged for hours. Every once in a while the keychain radiation alarm would sound, but only two or three chirps before it went silent again. Catching a lag in the storm, Sven got out and used the bathroom, getting back inside the truck just as the rain and hail began again.

He drank a bit of water and had a couple of handfuls of Gorp that he kept handy in the truck. It was still raining when Sven woke up the next morning. He hurriedly went to the bathroom in the rain after starting up the Suburban so it could warm up. The temperature had dropped significantly during the night and the rain was verging on freezing rain and sleet.

Another couple of handfuls of Gorp and a long drink of water, and Sven put the Suburban in gear and got back onto the road. The borrow ditches were full of water, sometimes covering the road two or three inches deep. Sven left US 160 west of West Plains and turned north, again wondering if he would run into heavy radiation further north.

The rain continued the entire time, actually turning to sleet as Sven went north. It quickly turned to heavy snow and Sven reduced his speed even more. He didn't want to come up on one of the abandoned vehicles on US 67 and hit it due to lack of visibility.

The radiation alarm began to chirp, very slowly and Sven tensed up some. But he was only a few miles from crossing the Wappapello at the north end of the lake and turning back south to get to his retreat. He pressed on, keeping his speed low, but marginally faster.

When he crossed south of Greenville and turned back south on county roads the alarm slowed down more and finally quit beeping altogether. Sven breathed another sigh of relief. Another three hours of slow going on the back roads and Sven was near his retreat.

As soon as he saw the gate blocking the dirt track leading to his property Sven knew there was trouble ahead. The gate was standing wide open. Though not locked, the latch mechanism was rather complex. An animal couldn't get it open and it sure wouldn't open on its own. Someone had been to the property and was probably still there. There was room to turn the rig around and Sven did so, going back the way he'd come.

When he got to the spot he was headed, Sven pulled off the road through a small opening in the forest and parked in a clear area a quarter mile off the road. It was already late in the afternoon and the snow was lighter, but still coming down. Sven wasn't in the mood to stay in the Suburban again or to set up a camp this close to the retreat.

A grim look on his face, Sven got out of the truck, pulled a pair of Carhartt bibs and a parka from the gear in the back and put them on. He shrugged into a combat harness of suspenders, belt, and pouches. He slipped the Colt into the holster on the belt, checked the six magazine pouches carrying magazines for it, and then checked the pouch of four twenty-round magazines for the PTR. He put the respirator that had been sitting on the passenger seat into a thigh bag.

With everything as it should be, with the truck and trailer covered with a camouflage tarp and the alarms set, Sven set off in the snow with the PTR-91 slung over his shoulder. He'd been all over this area on foot and knew exactly where he was going and how to get there unheard and unseen. The snow was actually an aid in his endeavor now.

It took him an hour to hike to the clearing where his retreat was situated. There were some signs of activity. He circled the entire area, looking for anyone that might be outside in the miserable weather. As expected, there wasn't anyone out and about. He checked the locations of all the caches he had around the area. None had been disturbed.

Sven went back to the clearing and approached the plain looking concrete block structure that was the basis of his retreat. There was a thin column of smoke coming from the fireplace chimney. He watched for a little while as twilight deepened into full darkness, with only the whiteness of the snow allowing any visibility that deep into the forest.

Backing away from the clearing, Sven went to get one of the cached shovels nearby. The ground wasn't frozen so it was easy to use his field knife to dig the thin layer of dirt from the shovel. It was a fiberglass handled shovel and the shovel head was well oiled and wrapped in plastic. It was in fine shape.

Shovel in hand, Sven moved to another spot, carefully checking his bearings. A few scoops with the shovel and a four-inch plastic pipe came into view. The end was capped. Another two shovelfuls and a plastic ammo can was exposed. Sven opened it and took out a battery powered fan and one of the six smoke grenades the box contained.

Sven slipped the cap off the pipe, pulled the pin of the grenade, set it just inside the pipe, turned on the fan, and set it so it would blow the smoke down the pipe. A little smoke was escaping, but not enough to matter. PTR ready in his hands, Sven moved to a position where he could see the chimney and the door of the retreat. He took a minute to put on the respirator.

It didn't take long. Thick smoke came billowing out of the chimney and people came rushing out of the small building.

In a prone position, the PTR on the bi-pod, Sven aimed at the only person that came out of the building with a gun in his hand.

"Drop the gun and I won't kill you!" shouted Sven.

Rubbing his eyes, the man fired the pistol at the sound of Sven's voice. Sven drilled him right in the center of the chest, turning the PTR on another of the four remaining people. "Surrender or die!" Sven yelled this time.

Though all tried to put their hands up, none could keep from coughing and rubbing their eyes. "Anyone else inside?" Sven asked as the small group moved further away from the smoke still billowing from the open door.

Before anyone could answer, another man came charging out through the door, a pump shotgun in his hands. Sven had to give him credit, the man was game. With tears streaming down his face and moving at a dead run, he still managed to get off three rounds of twenty-gauge buckshot toward Sven before Sven shot him, again with a shot to the center of the chest.

If Sven had been standing, at least one of the loads of buckshot would have hit him.

"Don't shoot any more, Mister! That's all of them! We didn't do nothing! They made us!"

Through the snow Sven finally made out that the remaining four were either women, or children. None were dressed for the weather, obviously. Sven got up and approached the group. "Don't try anything or I'll kill you like the others," Sven said.

"We're freezing, Mister!" said the same voice. Sven still wasn't sure if it was a boy or a girl.

"Give me a minute and I'll clear the smoke and we can go back inside. You'll just have to stand it for a couple of minutes." First grabbing up the two weapons the men had used, Sven ran back to pull the now empty smoke grenade from the pipe. He left the fan running.

Going to the building, Sven went inside carefully, the PTR at the ready. A quick look around in the heavy smoke and Sven went to a hanging cabinet, reached in and tripped a lock. The cabinet swung away from the wall, exposing an electrical panel. Sven flipped a breaker and the faint sound of a fan moving air could be heard.

When he went back outside, three of the group were huddled around the fourth. Sven stood there at the door, just watching, checking the inside of the building every few seconds. "Okay," he finally said. "I think it's clear enough to come back in. It'll smell, but you should be able to stand it. It wasn't tear gas or anything, just marking smoke.

The three helped the one and half carried what Sven could now see was a young woman, girl really, barely clothed. He grimaced. She probably was just about freezing. She was hustled inside and over by the fireplace. One of the other three grabbed a blanket from a pile on the floor and wrapped her in it.

"What now?" asked the woman after turning around from helping the other woman, and it was a woman, not a boy or girl. It was the same person that had spoken each time before. He got a good look at both of the others. There was another woman, and a boy of about fourteen or fifteen.

"Depends," Sven said.

"You try to hurt my sister like the others did, I'll kill you!" The boy was shivering, but stood tall when he made the threat.

"Your sister, you… all of you, have nothing to fear from me, as long as you don't go trying to kill me like those other two. Now, who are you? Who were they? And why are you trespassing on my property?"

"You should know," said the talkie woman. "Those guys said they knew you."

"Knew me?" Sven said, obviously surprised. Sven stepped back outside and took a better look at both of the men. He stepped back and started to go inside, but hesitated. He pushed the door open but didn't enter.

"Where I can see you, if you please," Sven said when he saw the brother, sister, and third woman, but not the talkie one.

Obviously reluctantly, the woman moved into Sven's line of sight. She held the fireplace poker in her hand.

"Now, now, now," Sven said, going inside and taking the poker from her hand without a problem. "You'll be a lot better off if you work with me, rather than against me. Now, I want some introductions and information."

"I'm Belinda Montgomery," said the woman that had tried to ambush him. "That's,

36

Traven Gregory and his sister Elaine...and my sister, Pru Conrad."

"Okay. I've got the names. What happened here?"

"What's the relation between you and your sister, and Traven and Elaine?"

"Coincidence. They were in the car ahead of us on 67 when all the vehicles on the road stopped running.

"Probably EMP," Traven interjected.

"Yes. I suppose," said Belinda. "For whatever reason, the cars stopped and we all were standing around wondering what happened. We were just this side of Greenville. A bunch of us started walking toward the town, but then those two goons...do you know them or not?"

"Unfortunately. A couple of hunters that ran across this place when I was here once. Not very nice guys and they didn't like it when I sent them packing."

"Well, anyway, we came up on them. Their truck had quit, too. But they were putting on hiking backpacks. They saw us, exchanged a look, and then pulled their guns. They were going to let the others go and make the four of us go with them, but Traven and Elaine's parents objected and they shot them. Everyone else scattered, but we were too close to them to get away. They brought us here. We've been here ever since." Belinda's eyes dropped.

"They… Pru and I…well, I guess you can guess. Why they didn't turn on Elaine until tonight, I don't know. We've all been expecting it. We were going to fight back, but…" Suddenly there were tears in her eyes. "One held a gun on us three and the other one started undressing Elaine. That's when the smoke started."

"I see. I'm sorry about your ordeal. How did you all survive this long? There wasn't any food here."

"The two guys had some camping food and one would hunt every other day. He must have been good. He brought something back every time he went hunting or fishing."

"Yeah. They were self-proclaimed expert hunters and fishermen. Maybe they were right. Moot point, now."

"They gave us just enough to keep us going, Belinda continued, "but that's all. Would it be all right if we ate something now? We are all starving."

"Oh. Sure. Eat up."

The blanket still around her, Elaine was given a bowl of plain meat soup before the others dished some up for themselves from the pot in the fireplace and sat down at the steel table that was bolted to the floor in the center of the large room.

The four ate ravenously, filling their bowls three times each as Sven stood there and watched, trying to figure out what he was going to do.

The same thing must have been on Belinda's mind. Finally setting aside her bowl, she turned to look at Sven again. "What are you going to do with us?"

"I'm not going to do anything with you or to you. You're on your own, as soon as I can get you out of here."

Belinda looked startled. Sven's reply hadn't been what she was expecting. She didn't really know what she was expecting, but that wasn't it.

"Do you know what really happened?" Traven asked, also setting his bowl aside. "Gerald, the guy with the shotgun, said we had a nuclear war. But we haven't seen or heard anything. Is it true?"

"I'm afraid so," Sven replied. "Don't really know how widespread, but I haven't heard any broadcast radio or TV since the attack. No Amateur's either. But there is less static now than there was. I expect to make contact any day now with other survivors."

"But won't we just die, anyway?" asked Pru. "People can't survive a nuclear war."

"Yes, they can," said Traven and Sven almost together. "You have survived," Sven continued as Traven fell silent. "It's a matter of continuing to survive that is the crux of the

39

matter. There are people out there more than willing to take advantage of others, because of it. But there are others that will be willing to help."

"Which are you?" Belinda asked, her eyes watching Sven carefully.

"I'm neither," Sven replied easily. "I'm not out to take advantage, but I don't plan on being that much help to anyone but myself."

"You helped us." Those were the first words Sven had heard Elaine say. The blanket wrapped tightly around her, she, like Belinda, was watching Sven carefully.

"I helped myself get back my property. I didn't do it for you. I didn't even know you were here. I was prepared to kill everyone in here if they were all in it together."

"But you didn't," Belinda said.

"No, of course not! I'm not going to shoot down unarmed innocents!"

"Okay. I accept that. But what are Traven and Elaine supposed to do? Pru and I might be able to make it home, if home is still there, but…"

"It's not really my problem," Sven said. "I plan on holing up here for a year or two until things settle down and then see what's going on. This is my home now since my house was destroyed in the attack."

"Did you get fallout?" Traven asked. Sven nodded, but Belinda was speaking again.

"Just because you knew of this place like those two men doesn't make it yours."

"No, it doesn't," Sven replied. "Buying the land and building the retreat myself does."

"Oh," Belinda said. "I thought… doesn't make any difference. If you won't help Pru and me, you have to help Traven and Elaine." She looked over at the brother and sister. "You have other family, don't you?"

Elaine had started crying quietly. Traven answered. "No. We have an old aunt that lives in New York City, but they would have hit New York for sure. If she isn't dead, she's having a hard time taking care of herself, much less us, if we could even get there and find her."

Pru moved over and began to comfort her.

"You can't just expect us to leave here, can you?" Belinda asked. "We don't have proper clothes since the weather changed and no more food or even any way to…"

Sven cut her off. "I'm not going to make you just walk out of here. I can take you into the nearest town. Perhaps they can lend a hand."

"And what if they can't?" Belinda asked.

"There will be abandoned houses," Sven replied. "You can live in one of them.

There's bound to be warm clothes just lying around."

"What about food?" Belinda swung her arm around to encompass the other three. "None of us are hunters. We don't have any guns. There is no way for us to feed ourselves."

"I can let you have some guns."

"We're not shooters. We're more likely to shoot ourselves in the foot than an animal. We wouldn't know how to prepare it, anyway. Those two men you killed dressed all the game. They made us cook it. We just put it in the pot with water in the fireplace and boiled it until it was done. We don't know how to live in the city without services, much less in the wilderness."

"So, I'm just supposed to take care of you out of the kindness of my heart? For how long? You think this situation is just going to blow over?"

"When you put it that way," Belinda said, her voice soft rather than harsh, "I know it sounds unreasonable, but we're just becoming to accept the fact of what happened. We didn't know for sure what it was. I thought it was just two guys taking advantage of a situation."

"I knew it was nuclear war," Traven said. "The minute the car quit."

"Okay," Belinda replied. "So maybe we did have an inkling of what was happening, but I don't have a clue as to what to do to be honest, Okay?" Belinda's lower lip was trembling.

"For crying out loud," Sven said, "Don't start crying on me." When her lip quit trembling immediately, Sven wondered if she was just playing him.

"We should just go take what we need," Traven said. "Like the two scum did. We're entitled. Give me a gun. I'll take care of us." He was looking at Sven.

"Taking from others because you have been taken from doesn't make it right." Sven studied the boy, wondering if it was just bravado or if he really meant it.

"Well, we don't have to take from people. Like you said, there will be stuff abandoned."

It made Sven feel a bit better but then he thought about what had happened in his own neighborhood while he was in the shelter. Everything edible that had been found had been taken. It was most likely the same, even in small towns, perhaps even more likely.

"Crimeny!" Sven said finally. "How did I get myself into this?"

"Come on," Traven said, rather insistently. "Give me a gun and some bullets and I'll take my sister to town. We'll make it on our own if you won't help us."

"Can't let you do that, Sport," Sven replied, "not in the middle of the night, anyway. Just plan on staying here tonight. I'll figure out what to do with you in the morning. Right now, I need to go get my truck before something happens to it."

"I'll go with you," Traven said.

"That's all right. I can manage on your own." Seeing the bottled-up emotion in the boy's face, having not been able to do anything to protect his sister or the other two women, Sven changed his mind.

"Though, on second thought, perhaps you should come with me. You know how to use a gun?"

"If you show me, I can," Traven said quickly.

"I don't think…" Belinda was saying when Traven cut her off.

"You aren't my mother! I'll do what I want!"

"Easy, boy," Sven said. "She's just trying to look out for you, whether or not you need it. It's your choice, as far as I'm concerned. You're a man now, like it or not."

"But…"

Sven gave Belinda a hard look and she fell silent. "From what you've said, you don't know how to use a gun, either."

Belinda shook her head.

"Then you'll get a lesson, too."

"You're going to give me a gun?" Belinda asked her surprise evident.

"As long as you assure me you aren't going to turn it on me. Just be aware that you're a lot better off with me here, alive, than without me."

Belinda nodded. "Very well. You have my word."

"Okay," Sven said and then looked at Traven. "Come on, Traven. Grab that coat and come with me."

Traven jumped to obey, not hesitating to shrug into the coat that had belonged to one of the men that had held them captive. Belinda, Pru, and Elaine watched as the man and boy went outside.

Sven pulled a Surefire G2 flashlight from a pouch on the belt and led the way to the exposed pipe and the fan still blowing air into it. He'd left the guns he'd taken off the two dead men there when he removed the smoke grenade.

"That's how you got the smoke inside?" Traven asked. "You planned for something like this?"

"Yeah. I'm a planner. As you can see, planning pays off." Turning off the fan, Sven put it away, re-capped the pipe and took a couple of moments to cover the hole again. "Which one do you want? Pistol or shotgun?"

"I think I'd better take the pistol," Traven said slowly. "Yeah, I think the pistol. The shotgun might kick too much for me."

"Good choice," Sven said and began to show Traven the workings of the pistol. It was a nice Beretta 84FS Cheetah in .380 ACP. Checking the magazine to show Traven how to do it, Sven found it still held seven of a possible thirteen rounds.

A few minutes later, satisfied that Traven wouldn't accidentally shoot himself or Sven, he led the boy back to the two dead men, carrying the shovel. They'd need it later.

Traven watched as Sven searched the two bodies. He recovered two spare magazines for the Cheetah and a holster. Traven slipped the Cheetah into the holster and put it on his belt.

There were an even dozen twenty-gauge shotgun shells with #6 bird shot.

"Let's go in and give this to Belinda," Sven said, moving then to the door of the building. "Uh…you first, Traven. I don't exactly trust Belinda."

Traven grinned. "But you're going to give her a gun?"

"Yes. Should make her feel better about the situation. Don't you think?"

Traven hefted the Cheetah. "Yeah. Yeah, I can see that."

The two went in. Belinda was sitting at the table with Pru and Elaine. Elaine had gotten dressed while the two males were outside.

As he had with Traven, Sven went through a short gun handling course with Belinda on the Remington 870 20-gauge shotgun. "Got it?" he asked finally as she worked the action a couple of time with the gun empty.

When she nodded, Sven said, "Load it up."

He kept a careful eye on her when the gun was loaded. He noted that she'd put on the safety, just as he'd shown her. Still, he kept her in his peripheral vision until he and Traven were outside and the door closed behind them.

Once they were well away from the retreat building Sven relaxed. The snow was still coming down. Sven kept a sharp eye on Traven. If he'd been on short rations, that fact and the cold might get to him during the long hike.

However, he trudged along beside Sven like a real trooper, occasionally putting his hands in his pockets, but usually swinging his arms in a stride to keep up with Sven's long legs. He never once asked how far it was, but Sven was glad to get to the Suburban. The boy was starting to fade.

Traven was able to help roll the tarp up and stow it, but sagged tiredly when Sven had him get into the front passenger seat. "Man!" Traven said as Sven started up the Suburban, "You've got tons of stuff! And this is a cool rig!"

"Yeah. Like I said. I plan." Sven got out of the forest and drove to the entrance to the property and pulled through. He got out and closed the gate and made sure the latch caught. When he got back into the Suburban Traven had fallen asleep in the warmth.

Sven was pleased to see he woke right up and alert, however, when Sven opened the door to get in. Another few minutes and they were back at the retreat. The two got out and Sven set the alarms and then joined Traven at the door of the building.

"Better announce yourself," Sven said. "Belinda might be just a bit trigger happy."

"Oh. Yeah." Traven replied, then called out loudly. "Belinda! It's me and the guy! We're back.

Sven leaned down and told Traven, "My name is Sven."

"It's me and Sven!" Traven yelled again.

"Okay, Okay!" Belinda said after she opened the door. "You don't have to announce it to the world."

"I don't think that..." Sven started to say, but fell silent when Belinda gave him a sharp look. She was carrying the shotgun, he noted as he followed Traven into the room. He hesitated for just a moment, but then hung up the PTR on a coat hook by the door, taking off the combat harness to add it to the rack.

"Door's locked," he said. "I think you can put the shotgun away," giving Belinda a pointed look. "You, too, Traven."

Traven yawned, but carefully removed the pistol from the holster on his belt and put it on what served as the kitchen counter. After a moment's hesitation, Belinda leaned the shotgun up in the corner.

"You'll have to sleep on the floor," she said. "I'm not going to ask Pru or Elaine to give up the bunks or the only blankets."

"That's okay," Sven said. He was on the verge of gloating, when he went over to the rough-hewn wooden shelving unit on the left side of the fireplace. He reached in and up, tripping a lock in the framework of the vertical member of the unit.

"I plan to sleep in a bunk. You're all welcome to have one, too, if you want." Sven was swinging open the secret door that gave access to the underground part of the retreat. Belinda started to protest, but didn't voice it, watching Sven.

Traven stepped over and stared down the circular stairway. Sven reached past him and flipped up a light switch and more of the room below ground level came into view.

"You've got a secret room!" Traven finally said. With a huge grin on his face, Traven looked at Sven and added, "More planning?"

Sven grinned back. "Yeah, well, planning pays off if you ask me. Wake the other two and come on down." He knew he was taking something of a chance turning his back on Belinda while she had access to the PTR, the Colt, the Cheetah, or the pump shotgun. But, although a bit tense, Sven went down the staircase with Traven hard on his heels.

Traven began to look around, wide awake now. Belinda came down next, looking around, too, but her look was one of bewilderment, while Traven's was one of excitement.

"You have a regular place here," Belinda said. "Electrical power...a kitchen sink."

Sven opened a door and Belinda looked in. "A real bathroom!" She looked at Sven, finally at a loss for words. Pru and Elaine were coming down the circular stairway, much the way Belinda had. Elaine headed directly to the bathroom and closed the door.

Traven was opening various cabinets and other doors, each new find drawing a "Wow!" from him.

"This has been here all this time and those two didn't know about it?" Belinda asked.

"Actually, no. While Traven got the Suburban, I built this." The humor was lost on Belinda.

"Sure. Funny. Ha. Ha. Why didn't your friends know about this?"

"They were not my friends, I tell you!" Sven said, a bit more loudly and forcefully than he intended. Belinda took a quick step back.

"Look," Sven said then, seeing the fear in the woman's eyes, "I only know them because they came through here, hunting, right after I finished this place. I wanted it to look like a hunting cabin, and it does. That's all they knew about, the hunting cabin part of the structure, and that's only because they were trespassing, not because I invited them up here."

"Oh," Belinda said. The stiffness seemed to slide right out of her for a moment, but suddenly she stiffened again, one hand going to her mouth. "You're a survivalist!" She took another step backwards, apparently more fearful of a supposed survivalist than a pair of renegade hunters.

"Crimeny!" Sven said. "I'm a prepper, yeah. I'm a survivalist by the old definition, not the new one that includes bigotry, anti-social behavior, and hatred of the government with the intention of overthrowing it. I made plans to deal with many possible emergency situations. Nuclear war was only one of them. One I thought was way down on the list of probables. In that regard, my planning was wrong."

"I think you planned great!" Traven said.

"Well, I didn't plan for you four."

It didn't dampen Traven's excitement.

Knowing exactly what he had in the retreat, after a short pause, Sven said, "Make yourselves at home…for the moment, but don't get too comfortable."

Belinda watched him as he went back upstairs to the hunting cabin. When he didn't come back down immediately, she went up the circular stairway herself. When her head cleared the floor level she saw Sven picking up around the inside of the cabin, straightening things up. He arranged the blankets on one of the four steel framed, steel mesh bunks and started to lie down.

"You're not sleeping down here? Aren't there enough bunks?" Belinda asked, taking another two steps upward.

"No. I need some time to myself to think. You all go to bed."

Belinda simply watched him for several more moments, and then turned around and went back down the stairs. A bit later Sven got up and banked the fire in the fireplace. He could hear the others downstairs, still up, talking. Sven shook his head, laid back down and went to sleep much faster than he thought he would.

CHAPTER THREE

-

As it turned out, he didn't have any better ideas the next morning when he woke up than he had when he went to sleep the previous night. Rather than possibly wake those in the retreat, Sven went outside and used the outhouse.

He was shivering when he came back inside. The snow had stopped, but the temperature had dropped even more, despite the cloud cover. It took a few minutes to get the fire going well again. Sven picked up one of the stainless-steel buckets kept in the hunting cabin and filled it with water from the pitcher pump on the kitchen counter by the sink.

After pouring a bit of the water into the cast iron kettle on one of the swing arms of the fireplace, he swung the kettle over the now roaring flames. When the water was hot, he scrubbed out the kettle and dumped it down the kitchen drain, rinsed and drained it again, and then put it back on the swing arm. He filled it with water from the bucket and swung the kettle back over the flames.

The water was just getting hot when Belinda, Pru, Elaine, and Traven came upstairs. "Why are you heating water in the fireplace?"

Traven asked. "There is hot water in the retreat, and how is that possible, anyway?"

"Don't want to waste resources. Yeah, there's hot water available, but I'll eventually be out of fuel, except for wood."

All four had the good grace to look sheepish, as each one had luxuriated during the long hot shower each took.

To change the subject, Traven asked, "Are we going hunting to get something for breakfast?"

"But there is plenty of fo..." Belinda started saying, but flushed and fell silent. There was plenty of food in the retreat, but Sven had a point. It would run out soon enough, especially if the four of them stayed. It was obvious that Sven had created the retreat with more than one person in mind, but she had to wonder if the additional occupants would have brought their own supplies.

"No," Sven said. "Go ahead and fix something for yourselves for breakfast. I want to get the bodies buried before they draw scavengers."

Pru and Elaine looked a bit ill suddenly, when Sven mentioned the bodies.

"I'll help," Traven said immediately.

"Okay," Sven said. "Let's go."

Traven hurriedly got into the oversize coat and stepped to the door. Before Sven had to remind him, Traven went over to the counter, picked up the Beretta Cheetah, and holstered it. Sven was doing the same, putting on the Carhartts he shed the night before, and then the combat harness. PTR in hand, Sven led the way outside, Belinda watching the two closely.

She shook her head and then turned to the entrance to the retreat shelter. Going down stairs, with the other two following shortly after, Belinda set about investigating the retreat the way Traven had the night before. The only thing she'd seen when Traven had been exploring was the pantry with food stocks in it.

Frowning, she looked over the contents of the pantry, but smiled when she found a cook book suited for the types of stored food Sven had.

"You going to be okay?" Sven asked Traven shortly after they went out and began to drag the first body toward the forest.

Despite looking a bit green around the gills, Traven nodded and kept pulling on the man's arm. Sven had the other arm. At a likely looking spot Sven stopped and dropped the dead man's arm. "There is a pick-mattock in the rack on the Suburban. Would you go get it, please? Here's the remote to turn off the alarms."

Traven's eyes widened in surprise when Sven gave him the remote with several keys hanging from its ring. "You trust me not to take off in it?"

"Can't I?" Sven asked in return.

"Yes, of course you can." A moment's pause and Traven added, "Thanks." Sven smiled at the boy. He was growing up very fast.

Sven had the dead man stripped by the time Traven got back with the pick-mattock. He looked a little green again at the sight of the stripped body. He handed the pick-mattock to Sven when he asked for it. Fortunately, the rains before the snow had started had washed most of the blood from the handle. Unfortunately, the moist ground had frozen during the night a couple of inches deep.

Marking out a rectangle on the ground, Sven set aside the PTR-91 and began to use the pick end of the pick- mattock to break up the frozen surface of the ground. With a layer loosened, Sven took a rest while Traven shoveled out the loose material. They worked that way until Sven set the pick-mattock aside. "Deep enough for these scum," he said.

Traven put down the shovel and helped Sven drag the body into the hole. They let it fall and didn't bother to try to arrange it any better than it had landed. The two took turns filling the shallow grave.

"We going to say words or anything?" Traven asked Sven.

"I'm not. Do as you think best."

Traven looked a bit uneasy, but finally just said, "Good riddance."

Sven hid his smile and picked up the pick-mattock again. Before he started to use it, however, he put it down and took off the combat harness and heavy parka. He was working up a sweat using the tools. That was dangerous in this kind of weather.

When the second grave was ready, Sven and Traven moved the body. After a bit of hesitation, Traven pitched in and helped Sven strip the body. He asked, "What do we do with their stuff?"

"In my way of thinking, anyone that attacks me, and I manage to defeat, their belongings are the spoils of war and therefore I will take anything I want that is useful. It's going to be a long time before industry gets back on its feet. Manufactured goods are going to be in short supply long before that. I don't plan on wasting anything."

"What about… well…" Traven held up the man's wallet. "Money and stuff?"

"Take it. You can have it. I don't think it'll be worth much for a long time, if ever, but you just never know."

Traven seemed to be thinking it over, and then finally tossed the wallet, still filled, over to the small pile of things from the other man. "I don't think so," he said. "You killed them. You should have their stuff."

"Okay," Sven replied. The two dragged the body over and let it fall into the grave, and then covered it up. Neither said anything when the grave was full. They just put their coats back on, gathered up everything, and then went back to the hunting cabin/retreat.

Sven wasn't that surprised when breakfast was waiting for them, but it caught Traven by surprise. "Wow! Thanks! I'm starving! I thought I'd have to fix something myself."

"Of course not," Belinda said, putting her hand on Traven's shoulder, but looking at Sven.

Sven added his thanks quietly, sat down, and ate at the table in the hunting cabin. The three women went back downstairs.

"Boy, this is good!" Traven said. "I thought I was going to starve with those guys. They just kept me around to bring in wood and stuff. I wish I'd had a gun then. They wouldn't have hurt Pru or Belinda." He put down his fork and looked down at the table, sightlessly.

"You did well, Traven. You did everything you could in the situation."

"I don't feel like it," he said softly. "They were hurting Elaine when the smoke came. I didn't even try anything then, just ran out with the others."

"Give it some time. You're a hard worker. Things will get better."

"I don't know if I can take care of the three of them if we have to leave here," Traven said, finally looking up at Sven. "Even with the pistol."

"I understand, Traven. Don't worry. We'll figure something out so you won't be responsible for them."

"I'll still be responsible for Elaine. She's my sister. I have to take care of her, even if she is older."

"Yeah," Sven said. "Well, we'll discuss it later. Finish your breakfast."

Both fell silent and did as Sven had suggested. They took the dishes down to the retreat and washed them, at Sven's insistence. "You don't have to wait on us, me," Sven said. "You're not captives now."

"As in, 'you're free to go. Don't let the door hit you in the…'"

Sven shot an angry look over at Belinda. "I haven't said anything like that!"

"Yes, you did. You as much as said that. You want us out of here."

"Well, come on!" Sven said, standing with his hands on his hips. "Are you telling me that you'd rather stay here, rather than try to get hooked back up with civilization? There will be a recovery effort."

"You think there is one now?" Belinda asked. She was standing aggressively, too.

"Well… No… Probably not yet… But…"

"If he doesn't want us, I think we should just go," Pru said, surprising her sister no end.

"What? This is the safest place around now. I don't what happened to you to happen again."

Sven sighed when Pru started crying and Belinda went over to comfort her. Elaine looked forlorn, ready to cry, too.

When Sven glanced at Traven, he was looking even younger than his fourteen years. Traven looked at Sven, and said, "If you really don't want us to stay, I'll take Elaine and we'll go. Can I buy some supplies? I'll have to work it off, sometime, but I will. I promise."

"Crimeny!" Sven said. "I do not need this!" He closed his eyes, pressed his palms against the sides of his head, and then said. "Okay. You can all stay until you make your own decision to leave…but I don't expect to have to take care of you. And I ask… demand… that you be conservative with the supplies and do some of the work around here."

"I will! I promise!" Traven said immediately. He looked over at Elaine. "Come on, Elaine. You'll be safe here. I can protect you now."

Elaine bit her lower lip for a moment, and then nodded.

"What do you want me to do first?" Traven asked.

"Clean the guns. One at a time. Come on. I'll get you the gun cleaning kit." Sven went over to the only door in the retreat that Traven and the others hadn't checked to see what was behind it. Primarily because the door was a vault door and locked.

Sven spun the knob back and forth and then pulled the door open and stepped in, Traven right behind him, his curiosity at high peak. Belinda found herself walking over to see what was behind the door that had been driving her nuts wondering what it was hiding.

"Holy moly!" Traven said after stepping inside behind Sven. "You got more guns and ammo than the police!"

"Not hardly," Sven said.

"Sure looks like it to me, too," Belinda added, also stepping inside for a look.

Sven looked a bit sour. "Well, I'm sort of a collector."

"I'll say!" Traven said then. He was careful not to touch any of the racked guns or stacked boxes and crates of ammunition, but he looked at each one carefully, noting brand, type, and caliber or gauge.

"Why do you need all these?" Belinda asked. "You can only shoot one at a time."

Sven turned around and gave her a hard look. "True…and the rest of my family and friends that were supposed to show up here if trouble started, would only shoot one at a time, too, in self-defense and in defending this place and each other."

"You… you have a family?" Belinda asked. "I didn't think… You came alone… I…"

"Here's the cleaning kit, Traven. Take it upstairs and clean your Beretta and Belinda's Remington pump. I'll show you how."

Belinda stepped back quickly when Traven took the cleaning kit and turned toward the door of the small walk-in closet sized room.

"I'm sorry," Belinda said softly as Sven came out, closed the vault door and locked it. "I just didn't think…"

"I don't want to hear it," Sven said harshly. "You've made your opinion of me clear enough. Think what you want. Come on, Traven."

Belinda went over to sit with Pru and Elaine as Sven and Traven went upstairs. "I think I really stepped in it," she told her sister.

"Yeah. I think you did, Sis, and for no good reason."

Belinda looked sharply at her sister. "That's harsh," she said.

"Yes, it is for a reason." She turned away from her sister and got up, going to the kitchen area of the large room to pretend to do something.

Elaine, uncomfortable with the situation, got up and went to the bunk she had used and began to make it up neatly.

Belinda continued to sit and ponder the situation. Had she really been that far out of line?

Traven watched closely as Sven showed him how to clean the various guns that had been used recently, and then went through the procedures himself.

"Okay. Very good," Sven told Traven when the guns were all cleaned and reloaded. "Now, in my opinion, you don't have to clean after every use, given only a couple of shots, but even if not used and exposed to severe weather, I like to clean them. Now, you up for some more work?"

Traven nodded eagerly.

"Take Belinda the shotgun, grab your coat, and I'll meet you outside," Sven said and got up. "I'll put the cleaning gear away later."

Traven hurried to do as asked and Sven put on the bibs and his coat before going outside to wait for Traven. He was in no mood to see or talk to Belinda. He'd been doing a good job of keeping the rest of his family and friends out of his mind. If they showed up, they showed up. The agreement had been that everyone was on their own to get here. No one was supposed to go looking.

At least, not while the situation was ongoing. After things settled down, Sven had every intention of going looking for his brother and sister and their families, along with two old friends that were part of the small MAG Sven had finally set up.

When Traven came running out, Sven had to smile at the eagerness the youth showed.

"What are we going to do?" he asked immediately.

"Have some stuff to cache. Things I don't want or need in the retreat right now, but want close and protected. I'm afraid it's more shovel work."

"That's okay," Traven immediately said. "My dad said work was good for a person, and now I owe you, so I have to work as hard as I can."

Sven had started toward the empty cache he planned to open up and fill. He stopped and turned to Traven. "No, Traven. You don't owe me anything. The situation brought us together. I did what I would have done even if you and the women weren't here. You help, pull your weight in general, and we're just partners in this thing until we have to split up."

"Oh," Traven was a bit subdued at first, but being called partner to someone who had what Sven had, even if only for a while, was too much to even dream for. He looked up at Sven's face and smiled. "Okay…Partner."

"That's the way," Sven replied, controlling the urge to ruffle Traven's rather unruly hair. Traven followed alongside Sven, more than just lagging behind the way he had earlier, carrying the shovel.

They stopped and got another shovel. Sven explained to Traven the series of caches he had around the area, without going into too many de-tails, or giving away the location of any of them.

When they reached the spot Sven was heading for, he took off his coat and combat harness, laid the PTR-91 on the coat, and began to swing the pick-mattock while Traven watched.

They both used shovels to dig out the loosened dirt. The hole wasn't as large as the graves, so it quickly became a case of taking turns, using just the shovels once they got through the thin frozen layer. With a domed fiberglass lid was clear Sven said, "Let's take a break and we'll go get the trailer over here."

Traven looked around. "You can get that trailer over here? I've got to see that!"

"Doubting Thomas!" Sven said and laughed.

After a short break, they walked back to the Suburban and got in. Sven started it up and pulled down the track that led into the small compound. He turned into what looked just like the rest of the forest to Traven, but was a trail carefully prepared to not look like one. The route took them well around behind the cache they'd dug open.

Sven parked the trailer beside the cache and looked over at Traven with a grin.

"Wow! You really did it! But how do we get out, now?"

Sven laughed. "Still doubting? You'll just have to wait and see again. Let's get busy."

Between them they removed the access hatch of the buried septic tank. "You're smaller. Down you go. There's a ladder for you to use." Sven said, pointing at the opening.

Traven didn't hesitate. He scampered down into the opening like a ground squirrel going into its den. "Wow," Traven said. "It's warm down here!" His voice rebounded inside the domed rectangle.

"Yep. Stay there by the opening. I want you to keep talking so I know you are getting enough oxygen."

"What do I say?" Traven asked.

"Just anything. I can tell if your voice changes."

"Okay. Can I sing or something? I can't think of anything to say."

"I don't know if you can sing or not. Give it a shot."

"Funny," Traven said in reply. He began to sing a popular tune. Even with the booming sound caused by the cavity he was in, he sounded pretty good to Sven. The singing stopped when Sven opened up one of the compartments of the trailer and handed a storage tote down through the hatch to Traven.

"What's this?" Traven asked.

"Just some stuff I want to keep. That one is some of my clothing."

"Oh. Okay."

Sven kept handing down totes, Traven asking about each one. It was enough to keep Sven apprised of the boy's condition. The movement was pulling down enough clean, cold air to avoid asphyxiation.

"This one is heavy," Sven said, maintaining his hold on the rope handle of the upper end as long as he could. He heard Traven groan when he took the full weight.

"What's in this one? Lead?"

Sven had to grin. "Sort of. More ammunition."

"Wow!" which seemed to be Traven's favorite expression, came once again.

"There is an expression about ammunition I try to live by," Sven said. "Buy it cheap and stack it deep."

He heard Traven laugh down in the septic tank. That was the last item to be moved and Sven said, "Come on up. That's it."

68

Seeing the sweat on the boy's face, Sven praised Traven for his hard work and the boy had really worked at it. Sven told himself not to let Traven's willingness and eagerness cause him to overwork the boy.

"I probably shouldn't say too much about what we've been doing, huh?" Traven asked as he helped Sven close up the open compartment doors of the trailer, and the rear doors of the Suburban.

"I'd just as soon you don't, Traven. I just have to ask you to trust me to do the correct thing. I'm not sure how the others will take some of my preparations."

"You did the right thing about letting us stay. So sure, I trust you."

It was a simple statement, but it meant much to Sven. The boy was right. Letting the small group stay with him, for the moment, was the right thing to do.

"Okay. Now you see how we get back to the retreat." Sven put the Suburban in gear and weaved his way in and out of the trees to get back to the tracks he'd made coming in to the cache site.

"Okay, so you did it again," Traven said, when Sven parked the Suburban. "Big deal. I'll be able to do that after I get a chance to explore some more." He was smiling at Traven's triumphant look.

"Yeah. Right. Now let's get cleaned up and see if we can find something good for lunch."

Elaine, Pru, and Belinda had prepared a meal from the stores that were available in the retreat. Belinda was quiet as they ate, casting the occasional glance at Sven.

Finally, as Pru and Elaine cleared the table and began doing the dishes, and Traven went to the bathroom, Belinda spoke. "About earlier, Sven… I'm truly sorry. You were alone…and I just didn't think about the losses you might have suffered."

Sven met her look. "Forget it. It's water under the bridge."

Traven came out of the bathroom and Sven stood up. "I'm going hunting," he told Traven, "to supplement the stores. You want to come along?"

"Sure!" Traven said. Then his face fell. "But I don't think hunting with my pistol will work very good."

"With enough practice, which we will get to, I promise, you will be able to hunt with it, though it still won't be the best option." Sven moved over to the vault and spun the combination knob. With the door open, Traven moved in right behind Sven.

As Traven and Sven discussed equipping Traven with a hunting gun, Belinda sighed and went to help her sister and Elaine with the domestic chores.

A few minutes later Sven and Traven left, after Sven carefully locked up the vault. Besides the pistol, Traven now had a Ruger 10/22 .22 rifle to use with all the accoutrements. He also had a Motorola FRS radio he was told to keep handy all the time.

Just before the pair left, Sven showed Belinda the radios and told her they would check in occasionally since they would be gone for a while. She simply nodded and Sven and an eager Traven left to go rabbit and squirrel hunting.

Sven carried the PTR slung over his back, and had another of the retreat's Ruger 10/22's. "Don't want to hunt close to the retreat in case we really need the food."

"I think the guy hunted just around here. He was never gone for very long," Traven said.

"Well, we're going to do it right. Hopefully there is still plenty of game between them and the fallout."

"Sven," Traven asked somberly, "Do you think we got lethal doses, not being in the retreat when the fallout came?"

"None of you are showing any signs," Sven replied, wanting to reassure the boy. "There was fallout north of here. I'm not sure there was any at all here. And, if you stayed inside most of the time, the hunting cabin would have given you quite a bit of protection. Its concrete block filled with mortar and the roof is six inches of concrete."

"So maybe we'll be okay?"

"I think so. Like I said, I haven't seen any signs in any of you of radiation sickness. But talking about this reminded me. I need to get another set of solar panels put up. The batteries are getting low."

"So that's how you have electricity in the retreat!" Traven exclaimed.

Sven smiled. "Yes. There are panels on the roof. Just a few. You can't see them from the ground, so, unless one were to climb up on top of the hunting cabin, you wouldn't know they were there. There are just enough to keep a good charge on the batteries in the retreat so power would be available immediately if someone showed up.

"I thought about hooking it up to some LED lights in the cabin, but I was worried that people would wonder about that and start looking closer. If you really study the place, it's fairly obvious that there is room on the fireplace end for the circular stairwell to be there. There were some other things I could have incorporated in the cabin to make it much more comfortable, but it was really just camouflage for the entrance to the retreat."

"It is cool. You did a good job."

"Yeah. It's doing what I planned for it, just not with the same people."

"Your family, you mean."

"Yes. And I'd rather not talk about them. We need to find a spot now and be quiet." Sven took a couple of minutes to lead Traven through the procedure of sighting the Ruger and squeezing the trigger gently until the rifle fired, holding the sights steady in the process.

"You may or may not get anything, since you aren't the one that sighted in the rifle. We'll get around to doing that, along with some practice with your pistol."

Traven beamed when Sven called the Cheetah 'his,' Traven's, pistol.

Both found a downed tree or rock to sit on, a few feet apart, and began to watch the area closely. Sven noted that Traven did pretty good at staying still, but he needed more practice. Sven had decided that they might as well go back to the retreat when he caught Traven out of the corner of his eye lifting his Ruger 10/22 to his shoulder.

Careful to turn his head very slowly, Sven looked over. Traven fired and Sven looked in the direction the rifle was pointed. Sure enough, a gray squirrel was falling through the branches of the tree it had been moving around in."

Traven looked over at Sven, a huge grin on his face. "I got him!" he whispered excitedly.

"You sure did. Let's go get him." Sven let Traven lead the way to the dead squirrel lying on the ground. It took him a few seconds to spot the squirrel as it had fallen into a patch of snow and gone below the surface.

"Careful, now, Traven," Sven said, putting a hand out to stop him from reaching down to pick up the squirrel. "Two things. One, sometimes they are just stunned, or just slightly injured. You don't want to just pick one up without being sure it's dead. They'll nail you good if you aren't careful.

"And two, always take a good look at the animal, looking for anything out of the ordinary, like patchy skin, sores or lesions, foam at the mouth…anything that might indicate the animal is sick, diseased, or infested with parasites. The last thing you want, especially now, is to catch something from a squirrel."

Traven nodded and watched as Sven bent down and brushed the snow away from the animal with a small branch he broke off the tree. "Eyes are open, and I don't see any movement of its chest, so it isn't breathing. Nice clean looking fur, no foam at the mouth or open sores anywhere. I think you got yourself a clean one."

Traven reached down and picked the squirrel up by the tail. "Uh… Now what?" he asked, looking at Sven a bit uncertainly.

"If we were going to wait and try to get another or two, we'd just set this one in a handy place and take up a stand again. But, since it is getting late and I want to show you how to clean it, we'll do that."

Sven slowly field dressed the squirrel as Traven watched. Traven only got a bit pale at the sight and smell of a dead animal being butchered. "Now," Sven said, holding the dressed squirrel out to Traven, "it's ready to be cut up for cooking. In the future, we'll probably start keeping the skins to tan, but I don't want to get into that right now. It might not be necessary for a while, depending on…Well, what we can salvage from abandoned homes."

Sven took a moment to lift the FRS radio to his lips and let them know at the retreat that he and Traven were on the way back.

The two were walking back; Sven letting Traven set the pace and the direction. He was pleased to note that Traven seemed to know the way back to the clearing.

"Isn't that stealing?" Traven asked. "The salvaging?"

"Depends on how you look at it. I consider it mining for goods, just as you would mine for minerals. Just manufactured goods in places where they've been left behind. Now, what I plan to do is only take things from places that are obviously no longer in use by the people that once owned them

"I would never take something from someone…only abandoned things. If someone has something I do want, I trade for it or buy it. Unlike some that believe that their need, or even want, entitles them to take something from someone else, I believe that a person is their own responsibility. If I didn't plan for something, that doesn't entitle me to take it from someone who did plan for it. If it's out there for the taking, then I'll take it. But, if it's marked in some way or just obvious that it belongs to someone alive, I'll leave it alone."

Traven had been listening intently but still managed to lead them, without thinking about it, to the clearing. "You said buy things," he said, "but you also said money probably isn't worth anything."

"I expect trading and bartering will be the primary type of commerce for a while. But something will become a recognized and accepted currency by most, simply because a currency makes exchanging goods so much easier. Before, some thought that ammunition, along with several other things would be that currency. Personally, while I have plenty of all those, I think real silver and gold coins will make a comeback as currency, at least eventually, and for some things."

"Wow," Traven said softly. "Elaine and I... We don't have anything to trade."

"Sure, you do," Sven said. "For the moment, just your labor, but as you work you'll accumulate things that can be used in trade. And assuming you'll be going on a salvage run or two, you should be able to find some tradable things for you and your sister, in addition to getting many of the things you want and need, just salvaging."

"Oh. Okay. That makes me feel better."

"Good. Here we are. You can clean the Ruger to get familiar with it, or wait, since you only shot it once. Whichever you do stow it in the locker that goes with the bunk you're using."

"Okay. Thanks, Sven," Traven said, ready to go inside. When it was obvious that Sven wasn't coming in, Traven asked about it.

"I want to do a walk around the place. See if anyone has been around lately. It looks like snow again and it will cover any tracks that have been made. I'll take you on a round sometime, but right now I want to get it done quickly. Okay?"

Traven nodded. "Sure. I'll take this in."

Sven handed Traven the Ruger he'd carried. "Hang my Ruger up on the hook inside the door. I'll put it away when I get back."

"Yes, sir."

"You don't have to call me 'sir,'" Sven said. "Sven will do."

"Okay. Thanks."

Traven went in, and Sven moved off to take a walk around the area.

It was full dark when he came back and went into the hunting cabin. Traven was sitting by the fireplace, reading the Ruger manual when Sven came in.

"I started a fire," Traven said. "I hope that's okay. I'll help cut some more wood. There is still a lot in the original pile."

"Sure," Sven replied. "It's nice to have a fire."

"Did you see anything out there?"

"Nope. Which is good. The snow just started. All of our tracks should be covered by morning."

Traven nodded and Sven took off his Carhartt outerwear and hung it up, along with the PTR and combat harness.

Other than Traven's eager explanation of the hunting trip to his sister, there was little talk during supper and just afterwards. Elaine had found the cabinet with the collection of DVD's stored in the retreat and asked Sven about watching a movie.

"Sure," he replied. "There's popcorn, if you haven't already found it."

"We found it," Belinda said, getting up to prepare it. She noted that Sven went upstairs before they had the movie ready. All she could do was sigh in exasperation. He was the most obstinate man she'd ever met, even considering the circumstances.

When she went upstairs a few minutes later with a bowl of the popcorn for him, she saw him already in the bunk he was using, apparently sound asleep. The fire was banked and the door to the outside was locked. She carried the popcorn back down and added it back to the big bowl the others were sharing.

Sven wasn't asleep. Close, but not quite. He'd seen Belinda through slitted eyelids. He just couldn't figure her out. With a sigh, much like Belinda's, he rolled over to face the wall and went to sleep.

The snow, while heavy during the night, had stopped the next morning when Sven got up and took a look outside. Everything looked pristine. If there had not just been a nuclear war, the effect would have been magnificent. But with the situation being what it was, the sight was simply noteworthy. Sven had wanted the tracks hidden, but hadn't needed the deep snow that came.

Traven helped Sven get out another set of solar panels from the storage room in the retreat. Sven asked Pru and Belinda to lend a hand getting the large, heavy panels up onto the roof and mounted. While they were moving the panels, Traven was clearing the roof of the cabin of snow.

Though Traven helped where he could, it was primarily the three adults that did the major portion of the work.

That was the way the next few days went, with everyone pitching in and helping Sven bring the cabin, retreat, and surrounding area up to its potential with stored items brought out and installed.

It began warming immediately after the last snowstorm, and by the time Sven had accomplished what he'd set out to do, there was only some snow left, in shaded areas on the north sides of things.

During the evening meal Sven brought up going on a trip to the nearest town to see what they could find out. Though Elaine, Pru, Belinda, and Traven to a small extent, had been listening for transmissions on the communications gear in the retreat, there had been no contacts with anyone in the immediate area.

All had been cheered, however, with the contacts they did make. Talking to other actual survivors of the war was much better than just accepting that they were out there somewhere.

At Sven's announcement that he was going exploring the next day, Traven eagerly volunteered to go along.

"Sorry, sport. I want you here to keep an eye on the place."

Somewhat disappointed, Sven's trust in him to watch the place made up for it.

"I just need one other person to go to watch my back." He was looking at Belinda. "You think you could do that?"

Belinda frowned. "Yes. I suppose I can. Do we really have to go?"

"You all need clothing, especially winter clothing. I'd like to find any food that is left that isn't ruined before it is ruined. I want to contact someone in the area if there is anyone. But I've already run into hostility before and it's safer if I have someone backing me up."

"I said I would do it," Belinda said firmly.

"First thing in the morning after breakfast," Sven said and got up. "I'm going to take a turn around the place."

Traven started to ask to join, but decided that Sven probably wanted to be alone. Then he started to say something to Belinda, but seeing the look on her face decided not to. Instead, he went over to Elaine and tried to get a list of things she might want Sven to look for. But Elaine didn't want to tell him. "I'll tell Belinda. She can look for me."

"Okay. Just trying to help."

"I know. It's just… it's girl stuff… and you're a boy…"

"I got it," Traven said, reddening slightly. With nothing better to do, Traven found a book to read of the large selection in the bookcase covering one area of one wall. He went to his bunk and lay down, switching on the LED lamp over his head to have light to read by. It was a book Sven had suggested he read, considering the situation, so Traven opened up the copy of the "SAS Survival Handbook" and began to read. He fell asleep with the book open on his chest.

With the trailer parked in its spot beside the hunting cabin, and breakfast in their bellies, Sven and Belinda left the compound the next morning. She had the Remington 20-gauge pump and a pair of six-round leather shell holders with extra shells. She didn't look particularly happy, but she wasn't complaining, Sven was pleased to note.

Belinda stayed silent on the trip, until they got to the edge of the Greenville. "My lord! What could have happened?"

Sven stopped the Suburban and they both surveyed the remains of the small town. "Looks like there was a fire and it got out of hand. I've got a feeling no one is here, but keep a sharp eye out."

Traveling slowly, Sven drove down the main street of the small town, weaving between cars sitting in the street and the remains of some of the burned buildings that had fallen outward. Not everything was burned to the ground in the small business section of the town, but it was close.

"From the looks of the snow that is left here and there, I'd say this happened a long time ago. Probably right after or during the night of the attack. Something caught fire, they couldn't get the equipment to run, and the fire just ran its course. Let's drift through some of the residential sections and see if we can find anyone. Keep that shotgun handy," Sven said.

They drove back and forth through the town, seeing nothing moving anywhere, not even a stray dog. Having checked every street, Sven stopped at the far end of town. "Climb over," Sven said, opening the driver's door. "I want you to drive while I check a few things out," he added as he stepped to the ground.

Belinda climbed over the custom console of the Suburban and settled behind the wheel. "Are you sure we should be doing this?"

"Yes," Sven said. "Do you have a list of things to look for?"

Belinda reached into her shirt pocket and pulled out a folded piece of paper and gave it to Sven.

He saw the extent of the list and lifted his eyes to Belinda. "Okay… I'll see what I can do." With that, he turned and walked up to the house on that side of the street. He stopped on the porch and knocked, calling out loudly, "Hello! Anybody here?"

When there was no answer, Sven tried the door. It wasn't locked and he went in, but came right back out. The smell was terrible. He went back to the Suburban to get a respirator.

"What's the matter?" Belinda asked when he got close.

"Dead bodies decomposing. I couldn't take the smell." He opened the driver's side passenger door and took out one of the respirators and showed it to Belinda.

"Maybe you should just skip the ones with bodies," Belinda said, her face pale.

His voice sounding strange through the voicemitter of the respirator, Sven said, "I want to be methodical about this. Not miss anything important we can use." He turned around and went back into the house.

Belinda was getting nervous, her eyes darting around in the silence. Sven had told her he'd be shutting off the engine whenever they stopped, unless there were indications of danger, to save fuel, so she'd turned it off when he went inside. It was eerie sitting there in a dead town with none of the usual noises present in normal times.

She started in surprise when she caught sight of Sven in the corner of her eyes as he came out of the house. She looked more closely and realized he was dragging a suitcase with one hand, and carrying several long objects under his other arm. The PTR was strapped across his back.

When he got close she discovered that the long objects were all guns of one sort or another. He put everything in the back of the Suburban and went into the house on the other side of the street.

They did the same thing well into the afternoon, with Belinda keeping watch and Sven salvaging what he could from the empty houses. The back of the Suburban was full when Sven said, looking as tired as he sounded, "That's going to have to be it. Can you drive us back? I want to keep an eye out to see if someone tries to follow us. There were no signs in any of the houses that others had been in them since the attack, but I don't want to take any chances."

"Okay," Belinda said and started up the Suburban again as Sven took off the respirator and dropped it behind the seat. "Was it…was it bad?" she asked him, glancing at him for a moment before putting her eyes back on the road.

"Yeah. I can't believe so many people just sat there and died. Oh, most of the houses were empty. A few of them showing that the occupants gathered up a few things and left in a hurry, but there were three where the people just…died…without even trying to avoid it, from what I could see. There were even a couple of obvious suicides. It's so pointless. If people had just planned for something like this…"

"I'm sorry," Belinda said softly.

Sven shook his head. "Not your fault. It just bothers me that so many people died that probably didn't have to."

"Did you find what you were looking for?" she asked after several moments of silence.

"Yeah. Not everything on the list, but most of it, at least small quantities of it. There will be more when we come back. Though it's been really cold, much of the canned food is still good, and almost all the packaged foods. I think a lot of it will still be good for several days, but I want to get it while we can. I think the winter is going to get a lot worse. Soon."

"So we have to come back?" Belinda sounded resolved to the fact.

"Yes. And I think it's best if it's you and me. I'd just as soon Pru, and especially Traven and Elaine not have to experience this. If I find a couple of places with much stuff, I'll bring Traven in to help me. He wants to pull his weight, as well as get some things he can trade so he feels like he's making it on his own for him and Elaine."

Belinda started to protest, but stayed silent as Sven looked around and studied the mirror on the passenger side of the truck. He didn't see anything and eased back in his seat after he got back into the Suburban after opening the gate for Belinda and then closing it behind her when she pulled the Suburban through.

Traven was waiting for them outside, though he wasn't just standing in the door. There was a rank of freshly split wood by the cabin and Traven was adding the last few pieces to it as Belinda drove up and stopped.

"Did you find anything?" he asked when he got over to the Suburban so he could look inside.

Sven managed a smile. "Yep. Sure did. And no trouble. You want to help me unload?"

"Sure!"

"Let's just take things into the cabin to sort out before we take anything into the retreat."

Traven called to Elaine when he took the first box into the cabin. "Hey, Sis! Come help us unload!"

Elaine quickly joined her brother, and Pru came up a bit more sedately, but they all pitched in to unload the truck. Elaine caught Belinda by herself and whispered, "Did you find everything?"

"We'll have to look. Sven did all the gathering, using the list you and Pru wrote up."

"Oh. Okay." Elaine went back to carrying boxes and shopping bags into the cabin. Sven made sure to take the various weapons in himself, despite Traven offering to do it three times.

"First things first. You'll get your chance," Sven told him.

Traven smiled and went back to work.

For the next week Belinda and Sven went into town every day to gather up things and make notes about things they couldn't bring back with the Suburban. Sven left a few things in place for Elaine, Pru, and especially Traven to pick up on their turn in to help. It was all clean, abandoned housing. He made sure he checked every building first before he let Belinda do any of the salvage work while he rested. There was no way to handle all the bodies, so he was just leaving them where they were if they were inside.

Belinda quit giving Sven questioning looks when he brought out an item that she couldn't fathom the reason why he would want it. Each time she'd asked, he'd had a quite logical reason. "My mind just doesn't work that way," she told herself and quit asking.

Traven was ecstatic when he helped Sven clean out the house Sven stopped in front of when the two came in for the next to last trip.

Not only were there clothes that fit him, but whoever the boy was that lived in the house, he had a sister about Elaine's size. Traven took even more items for her than he did for himself…and he found plenty for himself.

It had been a well to do household before the war and the boy and girl had both been spoiled rotten in Sven's judgment, if the possessions still in the house and garage were any indication.

That included a toy hauler already loaded with two quads and two dirt bikes. There were four mountain bikes on hangers in the garage. Another trailer carried four personal water craft. Yet a third trailer held four snowmobiles.

Sven and Traven hooked the trailer with the PWC's on it to the Suburban, as that trailer had a trailer hitch on the rear bumper. The trailer with the quads and bikes was hooked to it.

"Good haul," Sven said on the way back to the compound. "We'll pick up the snowmobiles tomorrow. If we split down the middle, you still come out with some stuff to use and some to sell. Lucky that was the house we did on your trip."

"Yeah," Traven said, smiling. "About that. I have a feeling it wasn't all just luck, so thanks."

Sven didn't look over, but he smiled slightly. "Sure."

CHAPTER FOUR

-

It was good they hadn't waited to do the salvage operation. Two days after they brought in the last load, December fifteenth, the snow started falling and didn't stop until they were snowed in under nine feet of snow.

"This is not normal," Traven said, staring at the wall of snow in the open door of the hunting cabin. He'd had to use all his strength to push the door open against the fluffy snow. It was like something out of a cartoon or a comedy show. He closed the door and turned around to look at the others.

"We all might be here a bit longer than I planned," Sven said dryly. "Don't know if its global warming turning the corner or nuclear winter, but you're right, Traven. This is not normal for this area. Not at all."

"What do we do?" Elaine asked, more than a bit nervous. She moved over closer to Traven, Sven noted, not to Pru or Belinda.

"We'll be fine. This place was designed to hold more than this many for weeks. The only things I'm worried about are the air intakes on the roof and the chimney. They might just be covered. We wouldn't know it yet if they are. I don't want to build a fire until I'm sure the chimney and the air vents are clear.

Sven walked over to the open doorway to the stairwell. What the others thought was just a steel bar there for some reason, Sven moved and it opened out into a ladder going up to ceiling in the stairwell.

Sven worked the latches of the hatch and was suddenly covered in the snow that cascaded down on him from the roof. The others couldn't help it. They started to laugh and Sven let out a mock growl before he climbed out onto the roof.

Traven was right behind him. They were in a snow cave of sorts. Sven was crouched down, swinging his arms and legs around wide, knocking more snow down the hatch or just packing it down when he could.

"This way," Sven said. "Be careful not to step off the roof. We'll see if the chimney is clear first."

Traven and Sven swam, walked, and crawled through the snow to get to the chimney. Traven scraped his bare knuckles a bit when he reached forward one more time and found the chimney. He worked his way up and his head finally broke through the surface. Sven stood up beside him. There was almost a foot of snow bridged over the chimney and he cleared it away.

The two knocked the snow down the chimney." Got it!" Traven called down to his sister. They can light the fire, now."

Sven was clearing the snow from around the chimney and told Traven, "Go around it. There is an air intake on the far side, in the side of the chimney, it's just some of the same blocks like these but with open spaces between them in the grout."

Traven took a quick look at the chimney were Sven was pointing. The concrete blocks, though you couldn't tell it from the ground, only had mortar at each end of the block. Most of the side was open to the inner part of the block. "Goes down to the HVAC system in the retreat," Sven said.

"Neat!" Traven said and worked his way around, slugging and stomping his way through the snow. He hit a soft patch and his head disappeared for a moment, but popped right back up.

By the time both of them were back down in the cabin, their clothes were soaked through and they were shivering. "Should have geared up for that," Sven told Traven as they both stood in front of the now roaring fire in the fireplace. "You go take a hot shower. I'll take one after you're finished."

Traven didn't argue. He hurried downstairs to do as instructed. Much to Sven's surprise, Belinda had a blanket from his bunk and was throwing it over his shoulders. "That wasn't very smart, you know. Besides the danger of falling, you both may wind up with pneumonia, going up there in shirt sleeves."

"Yeah, I know," Sven said. "It was dumb." He hunched the blanket over his shoulders and put his hands out toward the fire. "I'll be dressed properly when I go out to get more wood."

"Pru and I will help. We have some outdoor clothing now. We should all be sharing all the work."

"Yeah," Sven said, "But I'm not a very good cook."

"That's okay," Pru said. "I'll do your cooking if you'll do my wood chopping."

Sven and Pru both laughed. Belinda didn't, cutting a censuring look at her sister.

"Lighten up, Sis," Pru said, seeing the look. "You know I'm more domestic than you are. I prefer the housework to the outside work."

Sven kept his mouth shut, and his eyes on the fire. No way was he going to involve himself in a sisterly debate.

"I still believe that…"

Pru cut her sister off. "Leave it alone, Belinda. I'm going to continue to take care of this household. You want to go hunting and fishing for our food, I'll not say a word. But I don't want to do it. I'm going down to help Elaine with lunch. Let's go, Elaine."

"Okay. I'd rather do this work, too."

"So much for the modern woman's independence," Belinda said her voice full of disappointment.

It was a quiet breakfast a few minutes later, after Sven had taken a hot shower. Traven could feel the tension and, like Sven, kept his mouth shut. He wasn't too surprised that Belinda bundled up and went with him and Sven when they began digging their way from the front door to the wood stacked along the side of the hunting cabin.

Despite her earlier words, Pru pitched in, as did Elaine, but neither went outside. Their job was to transfer the snow being dug out to the big kettle hanging in the fireplace to melt it down so it could be disposed of down the drain in the cabin's sink.

By the time enough wood was brought in for several days, it was well after time for lunch. Belinda insisted on helping Elaine and Pru prepare it. Traven followed Sven's lead and stayed in the hunting cabin and cleaned up the mess that had been made moving the snow from the door to the fireplace.

Two days later the battery bank charge was getting low so Traven and Sven went back up onto the roof with Belinda to uncover the solar panels. It had been hoped that enough snow would melt so they wouldn't have to do the job. Instead, more snow fell both days, though nowhere near the nine feet of the first big snowfall. It was slow, careful work, but together they got them all uncovered and back in working order.

Things settled down into a relatively peaceful routine of meals, clean up, and leisure activities. Traven continued going through Sven's prep library as fast as he could read. Elaine tended to watch movies, but Pru and Belinda were teaching her to sew so they could tailor some of the recovered clothing for better fit.

Sven spent a lot of time at the communications desk, talking to other survivors that had access to Amateur radios. More and more people were finding each other on the radio and Sven was placing push pins in two large maps, one of the US and one of the world, with information received through the radio. There was a pad with the pin numbers with the data for that location. There was still no word from anyone close and no news about Sven's family.

Fortunately, Sven's plans for post disaster operations were both effective and extensive. The five spent the winter snowed in. It was the following March before the snow had melted enough to get to the snowmobiles and Sven's trailer, which had a gasoline tank for the gasoline powered items that Sven had. It was treated for storage, and when put in the snowmobiles, they fired right up with no problems.

"Okay," Sven said the morning after everything had been tested out. "I'm going exploring tomorrow. Just the local area. I can't believe anyone has been anywhere close, but I want to know for sure."

Traven looked hopeful, but when Belinda said she was going, he knew he would be staying behind. Belinda hadn't asked. She had stated. Sven didn't argue, either. He could understand her need to get out and about. It was the same with him.

So, with two of the snowmobiles fueled and loaded with emergency supplies, and Sven and Belinda both equipped with radios, the two headed out to take a look at the post-war, post-winter, world.

They didn't see much, mostly just snow. They also saw some few animal tracks in the surface of the snow, mostly small animals. "I've got a feeling the deer population has been decimated," Sven told Belinda when they stopped on coming across the frozen, desiccated carcass of a deer trapped in the snow. "And if there are any predators left, they are going to be very hungry. And aggressive. Keep an eye out."

Belinda just nodded.

"This being the case," Sven continued, "Let's go over to the lake at its closest point and see what's what."

Belinda nodded and gunned the snowmobile when Sven did his, keeping track with him slightly to one side. They almost drove right over it. The lake was still frozen over, and the ice was covered with snow.

"Crimeny!" Sven said as he rode the snowmobile in a wide loop to get back to the bank when he realized it.

"What's the matter?" Belinda asked when Sven stopped and lifted his goggles.

"We just ran out over the lake. It's frozen, but with the snow cover it might not be very thick in places. We could have fallen through." Sven's face was pale.

Belinda nodded. "That would have been bad."

"Oh, yeah," Sven replied quietly, then, after a pause, continued. "This arm of the lake isn't very wide or deep. I'm thinking, with the chance of game pretty slim, we should start fishing to supplement the stored food. Let's go a bit further south to look for a good place to start fishing."

Belinda nodded, put her goggles back in place, and followed along with Sven as he turned to the south, staying near the edge of the lake, now that it was obvious where it was. He finally stopped at a likely looking spot, stopped the snowmobile, and got off. Belinda followed suit.

The lake had very little snow on it here, since there were openings in the forest on each side and much of the snow had been blown off by some of the high winds that had occurred during the winter.

Taking a Cold Steel Rifleman's Tomahawk from the pack strapped on the back of the snowmobile, Sven carefully checked the ice at the very edge of the lake. Belinda noted his cautiousness as she watched what he was doing.

Sven kept trying to break through the ice, gingerly, as he moved out further on the lake. When he finally turned around and came back to the shore, Belinda could see a little color in his cheeks now and he didn't look as worried.

"It'll hold for some ice fishing for a while, I think. But there'll have to be two people, with one on the bank all the time, with a rope connecting the fisher and the guard. If someone goes into the water, it'll be bad."

Belinda had to nod. It sounded logical. And she said so.

"Let's get back to the retreat," Sven said. He lifted the FRS radio to his lips and contacted Elaine, on radio watch, and told her they were coming back. She acknowledged and Sven fired up his snowmobile again. They were going straight back to the retreat compound and didn't waste any time.

Both Sven's and Belinda's eyes were bright when they came to a stop at the compound. The run back had been sheer fun as they ran at high speed, weaving through the trees, Belinda locked on Sven's machine like a wingman in a jet.

Both were ready for some food and a hot drink when they went inside. Traven hovered around as Pru and Elaine took care of those necessities. "What do you think?" Traven finally asked. "Anyone else out there?"

"I don't think so, Traven," Sven said, hanging up the Carhartt's. "We didn't see any signs of anyone. Even the game is going to be scarce. We went over to the lake and found a place to ice fish on the lake while it's still frozen. Going to add fresh fish to the diet in lieu of fresh game. Whoever goes will need to take a shotgun, too, I guess. Could be some birds available, though probably not many."

Traven nodded. It was obvious he'd be doing some of the fishing and would probably get a shotgun to go with the Ruger .22 and the Beretta .380. Satisfied, he went back to listen to the radio while Belinda and Sven ate and warmed up.

Sure enough, two days later, with Traven checked out on riding a snowmobile by himself, he and Sven headed for the lake for a day's fishing. There would be a lot of prep and only some fishing the first time, but Sven intended to do it safely.

When they arrived at the chosen site, Sven and Traven went about setting up a secure place for the shore person to sit. The rope to the fisherman that would be fastened to a tree near the watcher, with another short rope fastened between the tree and the watcher to prevent the possibility of the watcher from advancing onto the ice inadvertently.

Roped to the tree, with Traven on shore in the watcher's spot so he could reel Sven in if he went through the ice, Sven walked out onto the ice with the pick-mattock in hand. It took a while, since Sven didn't want to take off his coat and couldn't afford to overheat in it. He worked slowly, taking frequent rests.

He finally had a hole in the ice and was much reassured when it became obvious the ice at this point was plenty thick to hold them without problem. Sven went back to shore, put away the pick-mattock, and unstrapped the fishing gear from the back of the snowmobile.

Traven watched as Sven rigged the line and then went back out on the ice. It was incredibly boring, Traven found, just waiting and being on guard for predators, birds, and trouble on the ice.

But his and Sven's patience finally paid off. Sven soon had three fish lying beside him on the ice. They switched positions and Traven got a turn on the ice. It was already getting late when Traven caught his one and only fish, but he was ecstatic when they went back to the retreat compound.

The two discussed ways to make things easier and safer, one being to make sure and secure everything out on the ice to another line going to shore. They couldn't afford to lose any tools or anything else to the lake.

Belinda insisted on going the next day and Traven expected to be at the retreat again, but Sven surprised him when he said, "You and Traven go ahead. Traven knows the procedure at the lake so he's in charge there until you get a couple of days of fishing under your belt.

Traven perked up and Belinda looked a bit aggravated, but didn't protest. Traven made sure he had his newly acquired Remington 11-87 semi-auto 20-gauge shotgun, with twenty-six-inch barrel, along with the Ruger and Beretta when they left that morning.

Sven began the tiring task of digging the compound out from under the remaining snow.

The two returned at the end of the day with a total of seven nice fish for the table. It became routine, every few days to send a pair out to fish. Pru declined to go, but Elaine was willing. She went with either Belinda or Sven, as did Traven.

Belinda spent her days doing inside and outside work, insisting on doing everything that Sven was doing. Sven had to admit, there was no reason for her not to. She was physically able to do almost as much as he, and had a bit more stamina than Traven.

On the first really nice day, after the compound was clear, along with what the others discovered was an impromptu firing range, Sven took everyone to the vault to pick a weapon or weapons to use full time. Reluctantly Pru and Elaine both did so.

After the daylong training session, Elaine was converted to a regular nimrod, and Pru was comfortable enough with her selection of a Ruger Mini-30 Ranch Rifle in 7.62 x 39 Russian to be considered as able to help defend herself as well as the others and the retreat if it became necessary.

It was mid-April when Sven took the Suburban out of the forest to take a look around. Belinda was as ready as Sven to see what was going on in the outside world. Despite the now regular conversations with other groups of survivors, they still had not found anyone anywhere close to them.

They went back to Greenville first. Nothing had changed there. Sven turned around and went south to the next town. When they got to Wappapello, they found it much as they had Greenville the previous year. No sign of anyone anywhere. Some of the town had burned, but not to the extent of Greenville. But, as Sven and the others had at Greenville, someone or a group had salvaged much of what was left in Wappapello. They turned around and went back to the retreat.

Sven was at a loss as to what to do. He knew the five of them could continue to live at the retreat for at least five years, using stored food alone. Longer if they could hunt much, fish, and grow a garden using the tools and seeds he had stored.

The others didn't really know that and he didn't tell them. They all could see that the food supplies in the retreat cabinets were running out. All had been hoping for contact with locals. Perhaps FEMA, though Sven's expressed opinion of that organization quickly subdued any more comments about it.

"We have to decide what we're going to do," Sven said one day as they finished supper, shortly after the trip to Wappapello.

"I agree," Belinda said immediately. "We can't stay here forever. What if one of us gets sick? We need to rejoin civilization any way we can."

The others waited for Sven to respond. He hesitated a moment, and then said. "Yes. That's a good point. And I want to find out what happened to my family."

"Well, from what we've heard on the radio, St. Louis was destroyed. Pru's and my home probably was as well," Belinda said. "I think we should go to Memphis. That's the nearest city that we know has survivors around it."

"Belinda, you heard some of the talk there. There's a major turf war going on over the existing supplies. I have family in Tulsa. I say we go there," Sven said.

"What about Little Rock?" Belinda asked. "I have business contacts there. That's where we were coming from when the car quit. Maybe one of them can help us."

"That's a possibility for you two," Sven said, indicating Belinda and Pru. He looked over at Traven and Elaine. "What about you two? You have an equal say in this."

Traven spoke up immediately. "I'd rather go where you go. We don't really have anyone…" Traven looked at his sister. "Sis? What about it? You want to go with Belinda and Pru, or with Sven?"

Elaine bit her lip, as she was prone to do when under stress. "I don't know, Traven…"

Belinda spoke up again. "You should go with us. A young woman out in this mess… Even you, Traven, shouldn't be going around armed, doing a man's work, at your age."

"It's my choice," Traven said, immediately angry. "And I'll take care of my sister." He looked at Elaine, and then back at Belinda. "Only if she really wants to go with you, we both will. It's my duty to protect her until she gets married and then her husband can take care of her."

"Married!" Exclaimed Belinda. "She's only fifteen! She's not getting married for a long time, yet. And you're younger than she is. It isn't your responsibility to take care of her. Not in a situation like this." Belinda was adamant. "Pru and I can take care of her when we get to Little Rock."

"What if we go to Little Rock first," Sven said. "Traven, you and Elaine can make a decision there."

"You'll let us go with you, if Elaine decides she wants to do that?" Traven asked.

Sven didn't hesitate. There was no way he was going to give Traven any reason to think he didn't have a place in the world. "Yes. Of course, you can."

"Then I say we do that," Traven replied. "Elaine? Is that okay. Go to Little Rock and then decide?"

The others could tell she was thinking about it. She finally said, "Yes. Let's do that. Maybe on the way another possibility will come up."

It took a few days to get ready. In early anticipation of this day, Sven had made sure to acquire extra camping gear for the others during the salvage operation in Greenville. The Suburban, Suburban custom trailer, and one of the toy haulers were loaded up with the idea that only Sven would be coming back any time soon, with that a big if.

The retreat was cleaned up and locked down, the cabinet put back in place to hide the entrance. It didn't take long to tidy up the hunting cabin to the condition it was in before the war. Shortly after nine in the morning of May first Sven put the Suburban in gear and the five survivors headed for Little Rock.

CHAPTER FIVE

-

Sven circled north through Greenville to pick up US 67 to go south rather than through Wappapello. With the decision made to go to Little Rock, Sven pulled off 67 and bypassed Poplar Bluff, not willing to risk meeting any hostile elements, if there was anyone there at all.

There were several small towns along US 67 which they passed through with no trouble. There were some signs of life, but Sven didn't stop to investigate. After they passed through Hoxie, Arkansas, Sven left 67 and they found a place to camp in a nearby State Park.

Sven drove around the park before picking a place to set up their camp. There were signs that the park had seen heavy use before and after the attack, but there were no signs of recent activity. There were abandoned RV's, tents, and other equipment. There were also some human remains.

Sven made sure they were well away from the remains when he selected the camp spot. It was near one of the comfort stations. Sven supervised setting up the tents, and he and Traven gathered up plenty of wood for a fire during the night. Then, despite Belinda's and

Elaine's objections, Sven and Traven got back in the Suburban and left the camp to salvage what they could from the abandoned equipment.

Traven looked a bit ill when they returned, but cheered up immediately when Elaine asked if he'd found anything useful, he eagerly described several of the articles they'd salvaged. There wasn't anything of real importance, but there were things that could be traded away for things more useful for a brother and sister.

Sven was pretty sure the place had been gone through before, for there simply weren't that many things that he and Traven found. Sven let Traven claim it all.

A watch schedule was set up for the night and everyone but Pru, who had the first watch, went to bed shortly after the supper Belinda, Pru, and Elaine had prepared.

Nothing untoward happened during the night, and the group was up, breakfasted, and loaded up ready to go at eight the next morning. Back on 67, they continued south without incident until they passed the BeeBe exit off US 67. They came up on a small convoy of people mounted on horses with three horse drawn farm wagons.

Sven slowed down and paced the convoy for a while. They must have been seen, for one of the men on horseback turned around and walked his horse back toward them. Sven stopped and let the man approach.

"This is probably fine," Sven said. "But everyone stay in the Suburban and keep a weapon at hand." He turned off the engine of the Suburban and stepped out of the truck. He brought the PTR out, but slung it over his shoulder, as the man approaching carried a long arm of some type in a saddle scabbard and made no move to take it out.

"How do," said the man when he rode up and stopped his horse a few feet from Sven.

"Hi," replied Sven. "Everything okay?"

"That's what I was going to ask. Saw you come up, but you didn't make no move to go around us."

"Didn't want to spook the horses," Sven said easily.

"Well, just ease past. It won't be a problem. You going into Little Rock for the trading?" He looked at the second trailer with its load of a PWC, quad, snowmobile, and two mountain bikes. "The bikes will be good trading, but I doubt you'll have little luck with the toys."

"They aren't necessarily for trade," replied Sven. "But we are looking to do some trading with other things. Two of my people have contacts in Little Rock they're hoping to find. We've been up in the Ozarks since a week after the attack. Haven't found anyone on the radio closer than Memphis. Just took a chance that Little Rock was still a going concern."

"Sure is. About the only place around this area. Rest of us are spread out around, growing food for those in the city. We get a little fuel, and some manufactured items. The people there pretty much sewed up the city right after everyone lived came out from wherever they managed to survive the fallout. Maintain they had exclusive salvage rights to everything in the city. Wouldn't try to do any, if I was you. They're pretty hard on anyone they catch 'looting' their resources."

"Understood. Thanks. What's the procedure for going in to the city? We'd like to find some specific people, if we can."

"You'll have to pay a tax to get into the city. Then you'll have to go to the city hall and register. They've been trying to · identify survivors in the city and the surrounding area, in case the feds ever get their act together."

"I see. What's the tax? And, I'm Sven Denali, by the way."

"Brook Nating," said the man. He leaned down and the two men shook hands. "Pretty much anything useful. They aren't out to keep people out, or make much that way. Just want people with a real want to go in to do so. Things are tough."

Sven nodded. "We know that for a fact."

"I need to get back to the convoy. There're some bandits about. I'd keep an eye open for them if I was you. A running vehicle, with fuel, is a real find. Go ahead and come around us. Maybe we'll see you at the trade fair."

"Understood. Thanks for the warning. Maybe we will see you at the trade fair."

Brook turned his horse and went into a trot to join his convoy. Sven got back into the Suburban and explained the situation to the others. When they got to the roadblock keeping anyone on US 67 from entering the city that way, Sven stopped and stepped out again. A man in fatigues, carrying a clipboard, met him halfway.

"Name?" asked the guy.

"Sven Denali."

"How many entering?"

"Five. Three adults, two teens."

"What do you have for entry tax?"

"I don't have a clue what you're taking. We just came into this area."

"Can of food each, Silver dime each, 50-rounds of .22 each, 10 rounds 5.56, .308, .30-30, 12-gauge or 20-gauge."

"Two silver quarters okay, then?" Sven asked.

"That'll do it," the man said, looking a bit surprised there was no complaining or haggling over the tax.

"I'll get it," Sven said, turning to go back to the Suburban.

The guard tensed slightly as Sven reached into the driver's side of the Suburban and pulled out a single shoulder pack, and took something out of it. Walking back to him, Sven held out the two worn silver quarters.

"Okay," said the guard. "You need to go to city hall and sign in. You'll need city ID's to leave."

Brook hadn't mentioned that part. Sven wasn't too happy, but there wasn't much choice. He nodded. The guard handed Sven a simple map with the roadblock and city hall marked on it.

A barricade was moved and Sven drove the Suburban, with its two trailers through it. Belinda took the map when Sven handed it to her. "I know the city fairly well. We'll go see if we can find anyone at McNally and McCoombs."

Sven shrugged. It was as good of a plan as any. It took much longer at city hall than any of them expected. The registration process included a doctor's exam and a dozen forms to fill out. One was basically a listing of everyone they knew for sure was dead, and who was alive, and the whereabouts each was last seen.

It was getting late when they came out of the city hall, with a map and directions where they could camp in the city without getting into trouble. There was a faucet to get water and a row of chemical toilet stalls at the park where visitors to the city that didn't have relatives to stay with stayed.

The group was immediately surrounded by the curious and those looking to do some trading. "I'd lay off the trading until we get a feel for what is going for what at the trade fair," Sven told Traven and Pru when both looked like they were going to start doing some trading with those in the camp.

Sven insisted on a watch during the night, too, despite the overall security of the place. "I don't want someone trying to go through our stuff."

Belinda was resistant to the idea and Sven told her she wouldn't have to pull the duty. But since the others were, Belinda said she would do it. As it was, they stayed up late, exchanging stories with many of the others in the camp. The stories were all different, except for one thing. All were from areas that had received very little fallout, and all had suffered through the severe winter.

Elaine and Traven exchanged glances several times. There were several others like them—youngsters that lost their parents to the attack, or the aftermath. All had been adopted

114

into a family willing, and mostly able, to take care of them. Once, when they had a quiet moment, Traven told Elaine, "I guess we had it pretty good, considering, huh?"

"It seemed so terrible when we were going through it, but I think you're right. If it hadn't been for Sven and his plans and the retreat, we'd probably be dead now, even without those two goons that killed Mom and Dad and took us."

"Yeah," Traven replied. "I'm not sure Dad could have kept us alive, out there on the road. Things work out for the best, sometimes, I guess."

"When someone knows how to make it happen," Elaine said softly.

The next morning the group was up and getting ready to head for the trade fair grounds, as several more people came by to see the newcomers. It cost them an extra thirty minutes getting ready.

But finally, they were on the way, following several other late starters. Once Sven knew where to go, he followed Belinda's directions to the offices of McNally and McCoombs, a decorating warehouse firm. It was locked up tight.

"We'll have to try their homes," Belinda said, her disappointment obvious.

She took a wallet out of the backpack Sven had provided for her and found her address book. Belinda told Sven the address and they headed for the home of Melissa McNally. They were stopped two streets from the one McNally lived on. It was obvious why the street was blocked. The entire development had burned to the ground.

Sven turned them around and headed for Patricia McCoombs'. Belinda was looking worried. But she cheered up when they reached the house in question and not only found McCoombs, but McNally, too, along with six other family members of the two. It was a tearful reunion. Sven learned that Belinda and the two women had gone to college together, majoring in interior design. That's what Belinda and Pru did in St. Louis. Interior design. They bought much of their goods from the warehouse Melissa and Patricia owned together.

"Can you take us in?" Belinda asked after the reunion and introductions were made. "Not Sven, just us four," she said, indicating herself, Pru, Elaine, and Traven."

"Elaine," Traven said, moving over beside his sister, "I think we should go with Sven. I don't have enough yet to take care of us here."

"You'll be taken care of," Belinda replied, her disappointment obvious. "You don't have to stay with him anymore." She gave Sven a hard look and told him, "And you can have your stuff back. I don't need or want a gun here."

"If you wish," Sven said with a shrug. He looked at Elaine. "You're welcome to come with me, or stay. No hard feelings on my part either way."

Elaine finally looked at Belinda. "I want to stay with Traven, and he wants to go with Sven. Sven's taken care of us well. I don't want to start over."

"Traven," Belinda said. "Think about it. She's your sister. You really want her out there in all that? You'll be safe here. You won't have to work as hard. You can give up your guns. You'll never have to shoot anyone over anything."

Pru had been silent during the entire short debate, standing over with the other women. She walked slowly over to Sven and turned around, to speak to Belinda. "Not that it makes any difference to Traven and Elaine, I'm going with Sven."

"Pru! Don't be ridiculous! You are staying here. I won't have it any other way."

"Sis, you've been a good sister, I guess, as those things go. But I'm out to continue my life the best I can. I believe I have better opportunities with Sven than I do here. I don't need you to make my decisions for me."

Sven and Traven both looked at Elaine. Pru's announcement was enough to tip the scales. "I want to go with Sven and Traven, and Pru," she said, not looking at Belinda.

"I think it might be better, Belinda," said Melissa, as she stepped up to her friend. "I'm not sure we could accommodate more than one more. Two under hardship conditions."

Belinda was disappointed and angry. "Very well," she said, looking at Traven. "Be off and don't come back here begging, any of you." She turned around and walked up to the house, Patricia going with her.

"Melissa," Pru said, "I didn't want things to end like this. But you obviously will be better off without the rest of us. Take care of Belinda, won't you?"

Melissa nodded and hugged. Pru went back to the Suburban, and at Sven's nod of his head, helped him unload the things that Belinda had packed to bring with her. When the others didn't notice, Sven transferred a small fabric bag to one of Belinda's bundles he knew she would be into fairly soon. Trusting her to her word, the weapons she'd been using were left in the Suburban.

The others started to carry the boxes and bundles to the house and Sven, Pru, Traven, and Elaine got back into the Suburban and they left, headed for the trade fair.

"I'm sorry it turned out this way," Sven said, looking over at Pru, in the passenger seat beside him.

Pru looked sad, but lifted her eyes to meet Sven's. "It's for the best. I've been a dependent for Belinda for my entire life. I need to be on my own and make my own decisions. I have no doubt there are young people there that will be better off with her mentoring."

Sven just nodded. It was between Pru and Belinda. Forty-five minutes later Sven pulled the Suburban in with the others with operating vehicles at the trade fair location. There was a place for those using horses for transport, and another for those on foot or with unpowered means of transport.

"I want to do a walk through to see what's what," Sven said. "I need someone to stay here with the gear." He was proud of the fact that all three said they'd stay, but especially of Traven, as he would much prefer to go with Sven, and Sven knew it.

"How about if Pru and you, Elaine, stay while Traven and I look around, and then we'll watch the Suburban while you two look for things you need."

All three agreed quickly and Sven and Traven set out, each carrying only their handguns, according to the posted rules they read when they pulled in. Traven had a small pad and a pencil and took down notes of goods and what was being asked for the item. It was both for himself and for Elaine, so she could check the things out he thought she might want.

An hour later a disappointed Traven and a silent Sven went back to join Pru and Elaine. They had prepared a quick noon meal and all four ate and used the chemical toilet stalls set up for the traders.

Traven gave Elaine the list he'd made for her and then went to sit down in the open passenger door of the Suburban to get out of the sun. "Boy, people want a lot for their stuff, don't they?" he said, as Sven sat down in the seat beside him.

"Everyone wants the most that they can get. A few people will be firm on the trade. Others price things high intentionally to be able to drop the price some so the buyer thinks they're getting a real deal. And there is another thing…" Sven reached up between the front seats to get the single shoulder bag.

Opening it, Sven took out a small cloth sack made from the leg of a pair of worn out jeans. He tossed it up and down a couple of times in his hand. Traven looked over at the jingle sound.

"Since there wasn't anything to spend it on, I've been saving up your pay and Elaine's for all the work the two of you did at the retreat." He handed the bag to Traven and

Traven opened it. He saw the gleam of both gold coins and silver coins.

"But we were just doing our share! And you said the stuff we brought was ours." Traven said and tried to give Sven back the sack.

"I know. The stuff is yours and Elaine's. And I know you gathered up some things to trade with. But having cold, hard, cash can turn a deal around. Not everyone here is willing to take precious metals, but many are. It should make your shopping easier."

"I don't know what to say, Sven. Thanks."

"It's okay. Better count it, here where you can't be seen, so you know what you have. And I suggest you divvy it up into several pockets so you never bring out more than a fraction of what you have."

"I understand. It's like keeping your wallet in your front pocket so it can't be stolen."

"Same principle," Sven said.

Traven fell silent as he counted out and stacked the different coins on one leg. There were only a couple of one-ounce Gold Eagles, and three one-half-ounce Gold Eagles, but there were several quarter-ounce and one-tenth-ounce gold coins, along with four rolls of silver dimes and quarters.

Sven smiled when Traven put various amounts of different coins into his pockets, putting the majority of the coins back into the cloth bag. He took two more bags out of the pack and handed one of them to Traven. "For Elaine," He said.

Pru and Elaine didn't take as long looking as Sven and Traven had. As soon as they got back, Traven took his sister to the Suburban and gave her the coins Sven had given him to give to her.

Sven was in the process of giving Pru a similar amount when Elaine ran up and gave him a big hug and kiss on the cheek, turning bright red when she stepped back and Pru laughed. "You too, huh?" Pru asked, showing Elaine the sack Sven had given her.

Elaine nodded. She looked at Sven. "Can we go back now to get the things we saw we wanted?"

Sven nodded. "You and Pru go on back first. Traven and I will hold down the fort." When Traven and Elaine weren't looking, Sven lifted his eyebrows and nodded at Elaine.

Pru gave a short nod in recognition of his unvoiced request for her not to let Elaine go overboard.

The sun was getting low in the sky when Pru and Elaine returned. Sven was glad to see that both had been rather conservative in their dealings, including using some of their trade goods as well as the coins.

After a quick exchange of notes, Traven and Sven headed back into the trading area. A bit uneasy about doing so, Sven encouraged Traven to go off on his own. When the two met up again, Traven was empty handed.

"I don't know," he said when Sven asked him about it. "It just seemed that when I could get it, I didn't seem to want it so much. I'd rather save up for something really important."

"Good thinking, Traven. I'm proud of you."

Traven flushed, but managed a smile as he walked back to the Suburban beside Sven. "You didn't get much either, that I can see," Traven said after a few moments of silence.

"Same thoughts as you," Sven replied. "I'm pretty well set for the moment and didn't see anything I needed long term that might be hard to find in the future. I just picked up these few items."

Pru and Elaine had everything closed up, ready to go when Traven and Sven rejoined them at the Suburban. Sven got in and they headed back to their camping spot at the park, satisfied with the way the day had gone, despite the scene with Belinda.

Sven heard Elaine and Traven both laugh in the seat behind him. He glanced back and asked, "What's so funny?"

"We both got a little bag of candy for the other," Traven said. "And one for you and Pru," he added, passing the small paper bags forward, two for each of them.

"Well, that was sweet," Pru said with a throaty laugh that Sven had never noticed before. "Great minds think alike, I guess." She passed back similar sacks of goodies for Elaine and Traven, and put one on the con-sole between her and Sven.

"Okay. Okay," Sven said, with his own laugh. "I was going to wait until after supper, but open up the single shoulder pack. There's a sack of healthy nuts in it for each of you, as opposed to unhealthy candy which I will eat with relish, anyway."

They all shared a laugh and then fell to setting up camp for the night as soon as Sven parked the Suburban.

There was no reason to stay in Little Rock. They had done what trading they wanted. Sven was itching to find out about his family, especially after seeing how well Little Rock was doing.

So, packed up and ready to go early the next morning, Sven drove them out of the park and headed for the closest access to Interstate 40 West. Pru, while not as familiar with Little

Rock as her sister, was able to navigate them to the junction. They had to sign out, so the administration could keep a handle on how many people were in Little Rock at any one time.

They weren't alone in their exit. Apparently, they had arrived just on the right day to be there for a much larger trade fair than the usual local only affair. Quite a few people had come into the city for it and were headed back to their homes, hopefully after trades, sales, or purchases that suited them.

While Pru, Elaine, and Traven had picked up a few personal items at the trade fair, only Sven had done any significant bartering, trading off several of the weapons he'd acquired by right of spoils of war, and by salvage, since they weren't likely to be used against him. In return for them, and a bit of coin, Sven got his fuel tanks refilled with biodiesel, and some gasoline he got for a song as it was very old and caused more problems in engines than it was worth. With the PRI-G Sven had in stock, he didn't mind.

There was only one other group that had motorized transport and they were traveling at a pace close enough to the speed Sven wanted to go that he brought the Suburban to a steady speed behind them.

They passed a dozen other groups, on foot, horseback, in horse or oxen drawn wagons and carts, and several on bicycles. Then it was just the two motorized groups. When they turned off at the Conway exit, Sven found himself picking up the pace a bit. They still had to weave their way around vehicles abandoned since the EMP burst had fried their electronics.

"Should we be checking some of these vehicles for salvage?" asked Traven as they passed a Cadillac SUV parked neatly on the shoulder.

"I've got a feeling that they've been picked over pretty good by now, Traven, this close to the city," Sven replied. "We get out a bit further out in the boonies and we may."

Traven nodded and eased back in the passenger seat. He was riding shotgun while Pru took a nap in the rear seat after pulling the early morning watch. There was silence for a long time as they watched the scenery pass by, seeing no one else after the other convoy had left the interstate.

They took three days to get to the outskirts of Tulsa, even not finding anything worthy of salvage. Sven had kept the speed down to the Suburban's most fuel-efficient speed. Though Elaine and Traven didn't notice, Pru was sure that Sven went a little out of the way getting them into the city.

Tulsa was being run much as Little Rock was, the city being mined for useable items needed or wanted by those that survived in the surrounding area. Food was the primary product the rural areas had for trade for those things the city had.

Sven wondered if Tulsa was in regular contact with Little Rock. Things were so similar, down to the entry tax and registration. But Sven paid and they registered, and then Sven headed directly to his brother's house on the west side of the city.

It, and the others on that side of the street, was burned to the ground. Like so many other places, without fire department personnel, usable equipment, and water pressure in the hydrants, minor fires turned into major fires, until they just burned themselves out.

Sven had to check. He wouldn't let any of the others go over to what was left of the house. All it took was ten minutes. The whole family had been home, in the basement, when the fire broke out. Sven decided that they had died of asphyxiation before the fire got to them. That was better than believing otherwise.

When he got back into the Suburban, Pru reached over and put her hand on his shoulder. "I'm sorry," she said. Like Traven and Elaine, the look on Sven's face when he walked out of the remains of the house had told Pru the story.

"Let's find that designated transient camping spot and set up camp. There's nothing for us to do here, now." Sven started up the Suburban and pulled away from the curb.

"Your sister and the others," Traven said from the rear seat, "We'll go look for them, now, right?"

Sven shook his head. "No. They were all there together in an improvised shelter. I've got nobody left."

"You've got us," Pru said softly, squeezing his shoulder just slightly.

Elaine was crying, and Traven trying not to. "Shouldn't we bury them?" he asked.

"No. Not much left and it's too dangerous to try to get them out. They're okay where they are," Sven replied, his voice choking slightly as his words trailed off.

They were silent the rest of the way to the camp, and during what was now a well a practiced routine. It was a quiet evening, with Sven going to bed without eating. The other three talked for a while, but went to bed shortly after Sven did, Elaine taking her preferred watch, the first one, so she could sleep through the night.

Much to their surprise, when they loaded up and left the camp the next morning, Sven didn't turn toward the way out of town. He went back to his brother's house.

"Sven?" Pru asked, "Have you changed your mind about burying them?"

Sven stopped in front of the house, killed the Suburban's engine, and turned in his seat to address Elaine and Traven in the rear seat, as well as Pru. "No. But I can't just walk away from what is here. I set up caches here, for them to use if they couldn't make it to the retreat. There is no reason to lose that equipment and those supplies. Traven, get the shovels."

Sven turned around and got out of the Suburban. Traven exited on the other side and climbed up the ladder to the roof rack to get the tools. He dropped them down to Sven and came down to help with the digging.

It didn't take long. It was another water tank buried so the access hatch was a foot under the surface of the ground. Unasked, Pru and Elaine began carrying the totes, boxes, bags, and individual items from the cache location when Traven handed them up to Sven and Sven set them aside to reach down to help lift the next.

None of them asked what the containers held. The individual items were obvious. Sven checked the load out and had to smile. Even Pru and Elaine had become quite adept at packing and loading the Suburban and the trailers for proper distribution of weight and still have accessibility to anything needed.

The other three stood and watched, as Sven, the loading done, walked over to the edge of the basement and bowed his head. He stood there silently for long moments, but turned and joined the others at the Suburban, saying, "Let's go somewhere and decide what to do now."

Sven took them back the camp, though they didn't get out to setup camp again. Instead, Sven turned to look at the others as he had earlier. "Okay. I no longer have people here. If any of you have some place you think you will be safe and can make a go of it, I'll take you there, if it is at all possible."

There was silence for a few moments. Traven was the first to speak. "Sven, me and Elaine have talked about it a couple of times since Little Rock. We want to stay with you. Wherever you want to go, it's all right with us. Right, Elaine?"

"He's right, Sven. I'd rather stay with you, no matter where we go. I feel safe with you and Traven watching out for me."

All eyes turned to Pru. Her eyes were on Sven. "I go where you go."

Sven rubbed both hands over his face for a moment, and then looked each of them in turn. "I can't promise anything. My supplies won't last forever. We need to find a place to settle where we can grow some food, or do something so we can trade for food. I have some ideas, but there are no guarantees."

"You lead, I follow," Pru replied.

Sven's eyes were still on her. "By my side?"

"I'm agreeable," Pru said, her eyes sparkling.

"What's that mean?" Traven asked.

Elaine leaned over and whispered, "I'll tell you later. But for now, it means we're all going. Like a family."

Traven grinned. "Well good. That's settled, where do we go from here?" Again, all looked at Sven.

"No doubt it'll mean a lot of manual labor." None of the three responded.

"Okay, Okay, Okay. We're a group. But I really don't know where the best place is to go. I'm open to ideas."

"Who on the radio sounded like they needed some useful people?" Traven asked. "What about back in the Ozarks in the Branson area? There are some farms there, right? We talked to them sometimes on the radio."

"That's true," Sven said. "But I have some doubts about them. You know what the winter was like. The ones we talked to barely made it. They're talking about going south to warmer parts."

"Oh," Traven said. "I didn't hear that part of it."

"So, it should be south, somewhere, then." Pru looked thoughtful. "What about that town outside of San Antonio? Elaine? The one where that boy is you talk to sometimes?"

All eyes swiveled to Elaine. She colored slightly. "Hondo. He's outside of Hondo. His folks have a ranch there."

"You think they need any help?" Sven asked.

"Not really... I don't know... We didn't really talk about the ranch very much."

"I have enough fuel to get there and back to the retreat without refueling. If the three of you want to chance the dangers on the road, we can go check it out. If it doesn't pan out, we'll have to hurry to get back to the retreat before winter sets in, if it comes early and hard like it did last winter."

"I'm willing," Traven said immediately.

"I'd like to go, too," Elaine said, turning red again.

"I guess that leads it up to you, Pru," Sven said as the other three looked at her.

"I say we try. It's the best option we have, in my opinion. I don't relish another winter snowed in, no matter how comfortable it might be."

Sven responded by putting the Suburban in gear and they headed west.

CHAPTER SIX

-

Sven took a route well west of Oklahoma City, as it had taken a couple of nukes because of Tinker AFB. Lawton and Fort Sill had also been targeted so Sven stayed west of them, too. Twice his keychain alarm sounded and they were ready to turn back, but the sound faded before they made the decision.

Since the interstates mainly linked those major cities Sven kept to the back roads since it was easier to just stay on them than to cut back and forth to the interstates between the destroyed cities.

They saw very few people, and those they did meet were friendly for the most part. Some looked covetously at the rig, Pru, and Elaine. Sven insisted everyone stay armed, not wander off from the campsites, and maintain a watch every time they camped.

There were a few places where locals extracted a toll, but that wasn't that much different from before the war. Sven made sure to have some trade items for the tolls. He didn't want to get the reputation of having lots of gold and silver. Word was being passed by radio of them being on the move.

One good thing about it becoming known that they were headed for Hondo, was that Ben Limon finally heard about it and contacted them on the accepted US call frequency on the twenty-meter Amateur band.

They were traveling south now, making their way around Amarillo, when Sven and Pru heard Elaine's name on the Yaesu FT-897D. Pru quickly reached for the mike and acknowledged the call.

Traven shook his sister awake next to him on the back seat. Groggily she took the microphone. She snapped to attention when Pru told her it was Ben.

"This is Elaine. Ben?"

"Hi Elaine. We got word you were coming this way. Any chance you can stop here for a few days?"

"Would that be all right?" Elaine asked in return.

"Sure! We're okay here. We can put you up for a couple of days without problem," his voice lost a bit of it excitement, "but I can't promise more than that. Things are kind of tough."

"We understand," Elaine said. Sven had pulled over and parked and he was nodding to acknowledge Ben's words.

"Be really careful, especially as you get further south. There are some really bad dudes raiding places. If they see you they'll probably attack. Don't take any chances."

"Okay, Ben," Elaine said. "We'll be careful." She looked at Sven and asked, "When should I tell him we'll be there?"

"Don't want to give too much away. Tell him between four days and a week."

"Ben, Sven says we can be there in between four days and a week. Is that okay?"

"Uh…Yeah...that'll be fine. My dad says I have to get off the radio now and get back to work. I'll see you in a few days."

Elaine handed the microphone back to Pru and Pru hung it up. Elaine looked excited. "I can't believe we're really going to see Ben!"

"Let's just hope everything is as it appears to be. And keep an eye out for trouble," Sven said. "With things going this good, there is bound to be some trouble ahead." Sven's words were prophetic.

They were just south of Mason when Traven spotted at least one vehicle behind them, keeping pace. A minute or so later Sven spotted the road-block ahead. "Okay people," he said, bringing the Suburban to a stop in the middle of the road. "We've got trouble. They've got us pinned be-tween them. We can drop the trailers and make a run for it across country. Or we can stay and fight."

"They'll take everything," Traven said. "We can't just give it up like that. I say we fight."

Elaine looked scared, but held her composure. "I'll do whatever you three decide."

"It's just material things," Pru said. "Let's leave it and go. Maybe we can get it back, later."

"That gives me an idea," Sven said. "Traven, unhook the lead trailer and get back inside."

Traven wanted to argue but knew there wasn't time. He opened the door and hurriedly ran to the back Suburban. It took only a few seconds to get the trailer disconnected. He was breathing hard when he got back inside the Suburban.

"Hang on," Sven said. He turned the wheel and went off the road as the following vehicle speeded up. And, Sven was glad to note, there was only one. They were a half a mile off the road when the chase vehicle got to the trailers and stopped.

Sven had stopped and turned the Suburban back to face the way they had come. "You three get out and spread out and keep watch. I'm going to see if I can convince the bandits to leave."

As the others did as requested, Sven climbed onto the roof of the Suburban and opened up one of the Thule baggage transporters. Leaving the aluminum case inside the Thule case, Sven opened it up and took out the Barrett Model 82A1 sniper rifle. He spread the bipod open, attached the scope to the QD scope base, seated a magazine into the rifle, and settled in behind it, still on top of the Suburban, laying in the V of the side-by-side Thules.

Traven, Elaine, and Pru had spread out and were also prone. They could see the old white Ford pickup with at least two men in the cab and four in back. The men all got out and looked first at the Suburban, and then began to go over the trailers.

One man lifted a walky-talkie to his lips and was speaking into it when Sven fired the Barrett. Pru, Traven, and Elaine all jumped. The sound was tremendous. So was the effect of the .50 Browning machine gun bullet when it hit the man with the walky-talkie square in the chest.

He went down hard. Sven fired three more times in rapid succession, taking down two more men before they could react. When the other men took cover and began to fire back, ineffectively with the weapons they had at the distance they were shooting, Sven put a couple more rounds close enough to them to scramble for better cover behind the trailers. Both continued to fire at the Suburban, without effect.

Sven turned the Barrett toward those at the roadblock. He knew he managed to hit at least three people before all had dropped out of sight. Sven turned back to the four men around the trailers.

With the scope on its highest power, Sven sighted on the pavement under the lead trailer, knowing he was taking a chance of hitting one of the fuel tanks built into the trailer. Ricocheting three rounds under the trailer, he wasn't sure he'd hit anything until one man got up and ran for the Ford. Sven put him down with a quick shot. There was silence then.

"Kids, you stay here," Sven called down to them. "Pru. You drive me up closer. Stay low, have your head up just enough to see.

Traven protested, but obeyed. Pru got behind the wheel of the Suburban and eased it forward slowly. After advancing a hundred meters, Sven told her to stop and put her fingers in her ears. She did so and Sven fired the Barrett again. This time he heard a scream, faint at the distance, but recognizable.

Turning his attention to the roadblock again, he emptied a full ten-round magazine into it, again ricocheting a few rounds under the vehicles that made up the block. When a car began to speed away from the roadblock, Sven hastily changed magazine and put five rounds into the old car. It swerved a couple of times, but kept going.

"Sven!" yelled Pru. "The pickup!"

While his attention was on the roadblock one or more of those with the blocking party had made it to the Ford and it was backing at a fast pace away from the trailers. Sven emptied the magazine through the wind-shield and the driver lost control. The truck skidded sideways and then rolled over three times before coming to a rest upside down in the ditch.

Sven waited for over half an hour, watching through the scope on the Barrett for movement.

"You want me to go check while you cover me?" Traven called up to Sven.

Sven hesitated, but it needed to be done.

"Go slow, and be ready. They may be playing possum. If you see any-thing before you get there, drop to the ground and I'll take it from there."

"Yes, sir!" Traven replied and hurried forward. He stopped at the Suburban and took out his Remington 11-87 20-gauge shotgun and carried it ready in his hands as he made his way forward.

"Ease me up every so often," Sven told Pru. She did so, going only a short distance and stopping again so Sven could shoot if he needed to without the movement of the truck interfering.

Sven made himself relax from the tension that had built as Traven had advanced slowly and carefully on the trailers. When Traven reached the lead trailer he stopped and waved at Sven.

"Pull up some more," Sven said when Traven seemed to be waiting.

It must have been what he wanted, for Traven began to edge around the back of the trailer when Pru stopped and Sven waved.

Sven wanted to scream when Traven disappeared from sight and two shots rang out. One was a rifle and the other Sven was sure was Traven's 20-gauge. Two more shots and Sven yelled at Pru. "Get me up there!"

Pru gunned the Suburban and Sven held on until Pru came to a stop at the borrow ditch. Sven jumped off the top of the Suburban, grabbed the PTR, and ran around behind the trailer. He saw Traven spin around, bringing the shotgun up and slid to a stop, his hands up. "Easy, Traven! It's me."

"Don't come up on me like that!" Traven said. "I almost shot you!"

"Yeah. Sorry. Won't happen again," Sven said. "What happened?"

"You were right. One of them was playing possum and tried to shoot me, so I shot him. And there was one over there that shot, too. I tried for him, but he ran away and was out of range for the shotgun. See? There!"

Traven pointed to the figure that had just jumped up from the brush a hundred meters from the highway. Sven tried a snap shot with the PTR and missed. Bringing the rifle up to his shoulder, he sighted carefully and put a .308 slug in the man's back.

Sven then checked each of the bodies at the trailers, just to make sure, while Traven kept watch. They both walked the distance to the Ford. One front wheel was still spinning slowly. There were two dead men inside, one probably dead from one of Sven's shots, the other, from the look of his head down on his shoulder, from a broken neck during the rollover.

Traven seemed fine as they turned around and walked toward the road-block, each of them moving to opposite sides of the pavement. When they reached the roadblock and looked around they saw three additional dead men. That's when Traven's adrenaline ran out and he sagged to the ground and began to shake uncontrollably and throw up.

Sven just stood there with one hand on the young man's shoulder until Traven finally stood up. Traven pulled a bandana from his right hip pocket and wiped his face. He couldn't quite meet Sven's eyes. "I'm sorry. I just…"

"It's all right, Traven," Sven said. "It's a natural reaction. Killing a person, even as deserving as these were, is hard. Someone as young as you shouldn't have to be doing it."

"I have to do what I can to protect Elaine," Traven replied, a bit of color coming back into his face. "And you and Pru. We're all together now. I have to do my part."

"You have. Why don't you go and get Elaine and Pru. Get the Suburban hooked back up to the trailers. I'll search these guys and then…"

"That's okay," Traven quickly said. "I can help." To prove it, he set the shotgun down and began to go through the nearest man's pockets. "Should we strip them? Take their clothes, too?" he asked after a moment.

"They aren't worth taking," Sven said, searching another of the bodies.

Pretty much only their weapons and ammunition was of enough value to take. That, and a rather nice stainless steel Coleman cooler with the remains of the men's lunch. There were also three Stanley Aladdin stainless steel vacuum bottles—two classic 1.1 quart and one 2.0 quart versions.

The two saw Elaine walking toward them as they got back to the Suburban to deposit their finds. Pru was standing beside the vehicle, her Ruger Ranch Rifle in hand. "Is everything okay?" Pru asked.

Sven nodded. "Let us get the bodies out of the way and then you and Elaine hook us back up."

"You okay, Traven?" asked Elaine. "That was so brave, helping like that."

"Aw, cut it out, Sis! It was just something that had to be done."

"And it was done well," Sven said. Traven went with Sven to the other side of the trailer to search those bodies and drag them off the road. Traven checked the man Sven had shot out in the open. He hurried back to show Sven what he'd found.

"I think he must have been one of the leaders," Traven said. "Look. He had gold and silver, two radios, a couple of knives, and these…" He handed Sven the decked out Springfield Armory M1A semi-auto rifle. "But I only found one other magazine. But look at these!"

Traven took down the fancy leather gun belt he was carrying over his shoulder. "They're Springfield Armory XD .45's. Two of them." Indeed, there were two of the thirteen round magazine capacity polymer pistols. One in a hip draw holster and one in a cross draw on the same belt. There were three double magazine pouches on the belt as well, and a scabbard with a Cold Steel Laredo Bowie knife.

"We're lucky he didn't have a scope on the M1A. He might have turned the tide if he'd nailed one of us," Sven said, sending a shiver down the backs of the other three.

"You think you might grow into those?" Sven asked suddenly.

Traven looked up, his eyes shining. "You betcha! I can have them?"

"Add this to the package," Sven said, handing Traven the heavy combat harness that he'd found half under the trailer. "I think he dumped this so he could run faster. It's got another eight mags for the M1A and four for the XD's."

Traven staggered under the weight. "I think you're right, Sven," Traven said with a groan. "This is too much for me right now. I'm going to put this stuff in the truck."

Pru was ready to move the Suburban, with Elaine guiding her. Sven went to gather up everything at the overturned pickup. There were three jerry cans of diesel fuel, two of them full. Some wrecking tools, Sven broke into the vehicles that were locked, several more guns and knives. And to add to Traven's loot, a musette bag with additional magazines for the M1A. There were six thirty rounders in one side of the double bag, and three Beta-C 100-round dual drum magazines in the other side.

With everything loaded, Sven got behind the steering wheel again and drove forward. They didn't bother opening up the barricade. Sven just went down into the borrow ditch in four-wheel-drive to get around it and then got back on the pavement.

Sven got on the radio, informing anyone listening on the different frequencies on different bands, of the battle outside of Mason. There wasn't much response to the announcements, although a couple of people essentially said 'good riddance to bad garbage.'

An excited sounding Ben was on a couple of hours later, asking about Elaine. "I'm fine, Ben," she told him. "I didn't really have to do anything. The others took care of it."

"Well good. I don't want anything to happen to you."

Two more days and they were camping out just outside of Hondo. It had been too late the previous day to try and find the ranch. Ben said his father was security conscious and would prefer to meet the Suburban in Hondo and take them to the ranch rather than giving out precise directions. Sven understood that and readily agreed.

At a little after nine the next morning, a group of six riders met Sven and the others at the edge of Hondo and guided them to the ranch. The only contact was Elaine and Ben waving at each other, and Ben's father leaning down to ask Sven through the open window of the Suburban to follow them.

When they arrived at the ranch, Ben and Elaine disappeared. Pru, Sven, and Traven were asked to go inside for something cold to drink and a visit. Big Ben, Ben's father, shook hands with Sven on the front porch of the sprawling ranch house and introduced himself and his wife, Melinda, standing just inside the screen door of the house until everyone came in.

"Park your artillery there on the sideboard," Big Ben said, doing exactly that. He unbuckled a western style gun belt and hung it on a peg in the back board of the side board. Traven, Sven, and Pru had left their long guns in the Suburban, comfortable enough with the situation to do so. Sven and Traven set their handguns on the top of the sideboard and followed Big Ben the rest of the way into the living room.

A few moments later Melinda was serving tall glasses of ice cold lemonade to Big Ben and the guests. "Don't get many guests," Melinda said, taking a seat on the arm of Big Ben's chair.

"Won't have too much time to socialize," Big Ben said, after taking a long drink of the lemonade. "Harvest is on us and it takes everyone to lend a hand."

"We'll be glad to," Sven said.

"Now, son," Big Ben said, "I wasn't asking you to do that."

"We like to earn our keep," Traven said solemnly.

146

"How old are you, boy?" Big Ben asked, his eyes studying Traven.

"Fourteen, Sir. Soon fifteen."

"I saw you were packing. You any good?"

"Pretty fair with a pistol target shooting…really good with a shotgun and twenty-two. I'm still a little light to handle full power cartridges, but I've got a good rifle and pair of pistols I plan to be using pretty soon."

"I see. Target shooting is good, but a man must be ready to protect what's his."

"Yes, Sir," Traven said.

"He can handle himself," Sven said. "Helped take out the bandits up by Mason."

"Heard a little about that. That was you people, then."

Sven nodded. "Nearly got caught in an ambush. Had to fight our way out. Traven was a big help, just as Pru and Elaine did their parts."

"Well that's good, then. But about working here, I wasn't saying you needed to do that."

"We'd like to, Ben," Sven said. "Like Traven said, earn our keep while we're here. Maybe do some trading. We're looking for a piece of land around here to set up shop ourselves, depending on the weather. We were snowed in for several months last winter where we were."

147

"Yeah, the boy said something about that. Been talking to your girl even back then."

"Actually," Sven replied, "She's our ward, not our daughter. Elaine is Traven's sister. We wound up together after the attack. Same with Pru."

"She's not your wife?"

Pru answered before Sven could. "Not yet. We haven't found a legal authority or preacher to take care of the ceremony."

Traven noticed the tiny flash of shock on Sven's face and smiled. What Pru had said was as much news to Sven as it was to Big Ben.

"That's good. Don't hold with people together without wedlock," Big Ben said. "Right, honey?"

"To many problems without the ring that binds you together," Melinda said in reply to her husband's question.

"We got off track there," Big Ben said, "about our weather here now. It's more like when we had a bad winter in the old days. Last winter was like one of them. You thinking they might all be like that now?"

"For the foreseeable future, Ben," replied Sven. "I think there is going to be a major migration south in the next couple of years. Those that don't make it by then either aren't going to and have the means to stay where they are, or they're dead."

Big Ben stroked his full white beard, as Sven continued. "I'd like to get settled somewhere. It doesn't have to be around here. Maybe somewhere where there wasn't much radiation so crops will grow without too much problem, at least where we could grow a garden and some small stock to keep us going with a little trading thrown in for the items we can't produce on our own."

"That sounds good. I don't know if you could make it around here," Big Ben said, setting up a little straighter in his chair. "We're pretty much taking care of the locals like us. What one of us don't grow another does. Even have one guy pretty much doing biodiesel only. We don't use much here, but some of the places still use diesel equipment since the biodiesel is available. Not sure we could do with the competition."

"I wouldn't want to be a major competitor with anyone around here. I think I could find a niche that would add value to the economy, without taking any food out of anyone's mouth."

"What'd you do, before?" Big Ben asked.

Before what didn't need to be stated.

"I was a cat skinner. Mostly the initial dirt work on new highways. Did some cartoon illustrating on the side."

"Not going to be many cartoons drawn now," Big Ben said, a bit of dis-approval in his voice.

"Certainly not. That isn't what I plan to do."

"What then?"

"Just depends on what turns out to be a needed service or project. I have an information base and tools to do quite a number of things."

"But no hands on for any of them?"

"Very little. But, like Traven here, I'm a quick study and good with my hands. I can do most anything I set my mind to."

"Well, I'd have to see that to believe it," Big Ben said with a laugh. "So, sure, if you want to work for your keep while you're here, we need a couple of hands."

"What about me?" Traven asked.

"You was one of the couple of...you and Sven here. Don't have no work suited a woman."

"I do," Melinda said, standing up. "Come along, dear. We have supper to prepare."

Pru looked over at Sven. He shrugged ever so lightly. Pru smiled and followed Melinda.

"That sister of yours..." Big Ben said, also getting up, "She do much of anything?"

Sven could tell the question annoyed Traven, and put a hand on his shoulder, but

Traven simply said, "Yes, Sir, she can. She's learned to sew, and cook, and clean, haul wood, fish…"

"Whoa, boy! That's enough. Melinda'll find her something to do, I'm sure, if she can do all that."

"She can. You have my word," Traven said solemnly again.

"Man's word is an important thing. Might want to watch where you give it. Wouldn't do to get a rep that your word isn't worth much."

"His is, Ben. Now, if you'll show us what you need us to do, we'll get right on it."

"Well come right along! The barn hasn't had a good mucking out since before the war."

Sven saw Traven's shoulders slump, but suddenly he was standing tall when Big Ben looked around. "You ever mucked out a barn before, boy?"

Traven shook his head. "No, Sir. But it sounds like a good place to start. I think I'd like to own some horses someday. Even with biodiesel, horses and oxen are going to be very important for farming and transportation."

Again, Big Ben laughed. "Well, you sure got aspirations. I'll give you that. Let's see how well you can work toward achieving them." Pointing out a dozen pairs of rubber boots off to one side of the horse barn, Big Ben said, "Grab a pair that fits you. No need to ruin good boots."

With rubber boots on their feet, gloves on their hands, each one picked up a shovel and began the arduous task of cleaning the horse barn. "I got my own duties to attend to, boys. See you at supper time." With that Big Ben left them to the work.

Traven looked over at Sven and mouthed the words, "supper time?" Sven just grinned and ran the shovel deeply into the accumulation of straw, dirt, and horse manure. Traven did the same, dumping the shovel of muck into the manure spreader sitting in the middle of the barn.

They hadn't worked long when Elaine came to get them. "Melinda says for you to clean up and come to the cookhouse for lunch."

They didn't waste any time doing so. And they were still the last ones in the chow line to get a plate and have it filled in turn by Elaine adding mashed potatoes to the plate; Pru, slaw; a girl about Elaine's age, gravy; and Melinda herself adding what she considered an appropriate number of pieces of fried chicken. Traven grinned when he got an extra chicken leg over the identical amounts he and Sven had received.

"Boy's growing. Needs good nutrition," Melinda said, with a small smile at Sven's slightly disgruntled look.

There was no coffee or tea, but there was a copious amount of lemonade, plus lemon pie for dessert. The meal done, after a bathroom break, Sven and Traven went back to the horse barn and Elaine and Pru helped clean up the cook house and get it ready to start the evening meal.

Supper was much the same, except there were steaks, potatoes, salad and vanilla ice cream for the meal. That was when they saw Big Ben again. He stopped Traven and Sven as they were leaving the cookhouse. "Come on up to the house with your ladies when they're done for a chat."

Sven and Traven exchanged glances, but went over to where the Suburban was parked. "Maybe we better wait and see what he has to say before we set up camp," Sven said. "He may want us somewhere else."

That was essentially what Big Ben wanted to tell them. Where to park the Suburban and trailers long term, and where everyone would be sleeping. Pru and Elaine would share a bedroom in the house with twin beds, and Sven and Traven would have bunks in the ranch's big bunkhouse.

Sven and Traven wasted no time getting showers and getting to their respective bunks. While both were normally hard workers, it had been a while since they'd put in a day like this one.

Or the ones that came after, for three weeks while the round up took place, and the fields were harvested. The only days they didn't put in full days were Sunday's. Only the animals were looked after. Other than that Sven, Traven, Pru, and Elaine were at liberty to do about what they wanted to on the ranch.

Elaine, quite naturally, spent every spare minute with Ben. Traven was much the same with the horses, except for one Sunday when he went with the other hands on the ranch for some marksmanship practice. He was really tempted to take the M1A and XD .45's with him, but decided immediately he would only embarrass himself now, so he stayed with the lighter arms, with which he was proficient.

Sven kept the Barrett locked up, too. He wasn't afraid of embarrassing himself. He just didn't want to waste the ammunition. Pru found some time to spend quietly with Sven on those Sundays, discussing their future, and the futures of Traven and Elaine. The four of them had become a family.

"I don't think Elaine could do any better than marrying young Ben," Pru was saying on the third Sunday they were there, with no major work scheduled the next day.

"I know," Sven replied. "He has most of the good traits of his parents, and few of the less than likeable traits."

Pru laughed softly. Sven really hadn't taken to Big Ben. Big Ben was a bit too pedantic, and more than a little bigoted, both qualities that Sven didn't care for. He was a bit tight fisted, too. Everyone on the ranch was well protected and eating well, but there was little more than that. If anyone wanted anything special, they pretty much had to make arrangements through Big Ben.

Despite the early indication of reluctance to have them work, once he decided they could, he kept them as busy as any of the other hands. Only on those Sundays could Sven go out scouting for a piece of property.

Pru went with him both Sundays he went out to check out places that people at the ranch told him about. One of the hands claimed ownership of a large piece of land on one of the many creeks in the area slightly northwest of the ranch. He went with Sven and Pru to look at the property. That's what it was. Property. Bare ground, scrub brush, and grass. But it had a well. That was key.

Sven was sure he could take care of anything else needed, except getting a well drilled. That was a bit beyond his ken. Sven and Pru walked over the property. It was on a slight slope, toward the dirt access road, with the well on the highest point in one corner.

"What do you think, Pru?" Sven asked as they walked back to the Suburban, where Mel was waiting.

"I don't know, Sven. It seems to me that there is so much property around with no one to claim it, that you could just set up housekeeping without having to pay anything for the land."

"I know. But I like the idea of have a good deed on the property. Things will come back. It's possible that the land will revert to the government if there isn't clear line of ownership. Or the squatter may be able to keep the land, by paying the government for it. I'd just rather have that ownership paper handy when there is a government again."

"I see. Logical. So, how much do we offer Mel?"

"I think I'd rather see what he wants, and go from there," Sven replied.

When they reached the Suburban an anxious Mel asked, "Well, what do you think? You want it?"

"You've got a good deed on it?" Sven asked.

"Right here. I brought it with me." Mel handed the paper, protected in a Zip-lock bag, to Sven.

Sven looked it over. "Looks like you paid it off and got the deed just before the attack. Are you sure you want to get rid of it?"

"I've got to have food, or means to get it, for my family. I've got three young kids and a wife pregnant with another. I'm just making enough at the ranch to get by. I don't want my wife and kids just getting by. I want them to have more."

"You rather have food, trade goods, gold, or a promise of a job?"

"I've got a good job," Mel replied. He seemed a bit affronted that Sven would try to hire him away from Big Ben. "The other three, in combination are heavy on the food and trade goods, and light on gold. It's not going over very well around here."

"I can let you have two weeks' worth of food, for the family, every month, for three years, trade goods that would get you two more weeks' worth of food the way things are right now, and twelve ounces of gold, mostly in one-tenth-ounce and one-quarter-ounce gold eagles."

"What if you don't pay me every month? That sounds like a hard thing to pull off," Mel said.

"Same as used to. Land goes back to you. I'd like at least two months' grace on the payments before you consider taking back the land, if I miss a payment. And I'd like a discount if I can pay it off early."

"How much discount?"

"Whatever gold hasn't been paid, based on paying it four ounces a year for the three years.

"Let me talk it over with my wife. We bought the land from her parents. See if she's agreeable."

Sven nodded and the three of them got back into the Suburban. Sven dropped Mel off at his small place a mile from the ranch. Sven and Pru went back to the ranch. Sven parked by his trailers.

Pru went to the main house and Sven went looking for Traven. He found him the first place he looked...in the horse corral. Traven was grooming one of the colts. He seemed to have a knack with horses, and Big Ben had him working with his trainer during the week.

Traven saw Sven and finished up the grooming, and released the colt. It followed Traven over to the corral fence where he went to join Sven.

"I think you have a shadow," Sven said with a smile.

"Yeah. Lil' Crunch here is a pest." Belying his words, Traven rubbed the colt's head fondly.

"I need to talk to you. Serious stuff."

Traven nodded and climbed over the corral fence. "Problems?" he asked as the two walked toward the ranch parking lot where the Suburban and the two trailers were parked.

"Not problems. Opportunities, I hope. I found some land I want to buy. I need to cut a deal with you for some of your stuff, to use in trade to get some of what I need to get the land."

"Sounds complicated, but you know you can have anything of mine you want," Traven said. He put one booted foot up on the bumper of the toy hauler trailer.

"It is a little, and I'm not sure it would work. Big Ben has been making some noises about maybe getting the quad and personal water craft. He doesn't seem interested in the snowmobile, though I'm not sure why. Seems to me it would be the most useful, the way the winters are. Any-way, they're yours and Elaine's. What would you take for them?"

"Gee, Sven! I have pretty much everything I need on a day-to-day basis. You've seen to that. Why don't you just use them if you can and you can owe me?"

"I was thinking you might like one of the horses here," Sven said, watching Traven carefully.

Traven's eyes lit up immediately. "Well, Gee! Yeah! But I sort of hinted at it to Ben to see what his father would say. Big Ben, according to Ben, wasn't interested."

Sven kept his voice low when he replied. "I have to tell you, Traven, Big Ben has

JERRY D. YOUNG

some prejudices. I don't think he likes the idea of trading with someone your age."

Traven frowned. "What difference does that make?"

"To me, none. Not everyone feels the same way."

"Well, I'm fifteen next week. I think that's old enough to make deals on my own!"

"So do I. I think you're old enough now. That's why I'm talking to you."

"Oh. Yeah. So, what would the trade be?"

"You said something about wanting to have horses someday. Would one of Big Ben's horses now, and a colt or filly next year be acceptable for the two toys?"

"Shoot, yeah! Without much gas, I can't use them much, anyway."

"I was thinking that, too. You've been really good about not asking for any. Let me see what I can do. It'll have to be tomorrow. Big Ben won't dicker on a Sunday."

"Yeah, I know Sven. What about Elaine? She's half owner."

Sven grinned at Traven. "That's your own deal, there. It's up to you how you handle it."

Traven sighed. "Yeah. It is. Okay. I'll let you know tomorrow."

Sven waited another day. Big Ben wasn't very happy the Monday following

160

Sven's conversations with Mel, Pru, and Traven. But on Tuesday, Big Ben was his usual self and took Sven to the den in the house when Sven asked to talk to him.

"What's up? Not wanting a job over the winter, I hope. Don't really need any more than the permanent hands I have."

"It's not that," Sven replied. "I wouldn't impose on your generosity like that."

Big Ben grunted in acknowledgement, but didn't say anything.

"I was hoping to work a deal or two before I go north again."

"I'm listening."

"You said something about the quad and PWC here awhile back. If you're still interested, they're up for trade."

"You working this for your boy?"

"Nope. I'm trading Traven for them."

"So they are his?"

"His and Elaine's," replied Sven. "Like I said, I'm getting the units from them."

"What'cha asking?" Big Ben asked. He was always up for a deal. And he usually came out on his deals smelling like a rose.

"I'd need two horses, two steers, and two grown pigs."

Big Ben barked out a laugh. "You've got to be kidding me! Barely be able to use them. Don't have much gas."

"I'll throw in some gasoline. Been treated for storage so it's good."

The look in Big Ben's eyes changed slightly. "Can't do it. I need to build the herds. How much gasoline?"

"Hundred gallons."

Big Ben looked impressed. Even here in Texas, gasoline was hard to get. But he shook his head. "I'm trying to build herds. I need to keep as much of my stock as I can, butchering just enough to meet needs. And the horses… well, they're valuable."

"The horses next spring, say, a colt and a filly. One pig now, and one pig next fall, one steer next summer, and one the summer after."

Big Ben was showing some real interest. "Well now. You have made it interesting." Then he smiled. "But I don't think so. I'm having a hard time on a horse now. Be nice to have that quad to get around on. Used one for a while but Ben busted it up. But I can still ride my horse."

"That first one hundred gallons of gasoline now and a hundred next spring and I'll kick in a couple ounces of gold, to boot."

"You talk a good deal. You actually have that gas and gold?"

Sven nodded.

"Let's go take a look at them," Big Ben said, standing up and moving around the desk he'd been sitting behind.

Sven started up the quad and backed it off the trailer. He let Big Ben get on it and Ben took off with a whoop and a holler. He disappeared for almost ten minutes. When he got back, he shut off the quad, but didn't get off. "You've got a deal!"

"I have to ask," Sven said. "Why do you want the PWC?"

"I'll use it on the lake to fish from."

"What lake?" Sven asked.

"You haven't been out on that way. Got an irrigation lake on the back side of the property. It's loaded with fish, but they hang out in the deeper middle part. I'm not about to row a boat, with my back, nor ask one of the hands. With the PWC, I can get right out there."

Sven nodded. "You want to take it out there now?"

"Absolutely. But let's have that gas, first."

Sven hid his smile and hooked up the custom trailer to the Suburban and moved it to the Ranch's small tank farm. He pumped one hundred gallons into Big Ben's gasoline tank and then re-parked that trailer. With the toy hauler attached, Traven in the passenger seat of the Suburban, and Big Ben on the Quad, Ben led them to the lake.

Sven backed the trailer down the slope of the bank of the lake and he and Traven horsed the PWC into the water.

"Ready to go," Traven said, holding the craft against the bank.

Big Ben hopped off the Quad and onto the PWC. A few seconds later and he was leaving a rooster tail of water behind him as he circled the large lake.

"I've got a feeling he's not going to just fish from that thing," Sven said.

Traven grinned. "I don't think so."

Sven motioned to Big Ben as he passed by that he and Traven were going back to the ranch building compound. Big Ben waved them on, and turned back to the center of the lake.

As casually as he could, Traven finally asked Sven, "I know you made a trade. Was it a good one?"

"Oh, yes," Sven said. "Got a pig for right now; a colt and a filly next spring; a steer next summer; another pig next fall, and a steer the summer after. I had to throw in some gasoline and just a little gold to close the deal."

"Really? You got two horses?"

"Sure did. Both of them yours. Is that okay?"

"You betcha!"

"What about Elaine?" Sven asked.

"I offered her some of my trade goods of her choice, and a little bit of gold and silver. She let me have the trailer and all of the toys. She was happy. I think her and Ben are getting pretty serious. She might not want to go back with us."

"How do you feel about that?"

"I don't know," Traven said slowly. "She'd be better off here. She's been doing her part with us, but it's just not the kind of life she should have. I think if she marries Ben, it would be good for her. And me, too."

Traven was right. Elaine's sixteenth birthday was two days after Traven's fifteenth. Ben asked her to stay, and Big Ben and Melinda both agreed if Traven agreed to stay and be her chaperone until Ben got around to asking Elaine to marry him.

Two days after Elaine's birthday Pru and Sven were headed back to the retreat with the Suburban and the custom trailer. The toy hauler with Traven's snowmobile, two mountain bikes, and fifty gallons of gasoline in jerry cans was left behind.

Mel had his first payment of the land, to seal the deal. Mel made his own arrangements to get the first pig butchered and put up as the major portion of the first year's food payment. Another fifty gallons of gasoline in jerry cans was the year's trade goods payment, and Sven handed over four ounces of gold in one-tenth-ounce and one-quarter-ounce gold coins.

Sven had to drive through the winter's first big snowfall to get to the re-treat. He and

Pru settled down for the winter, to get to know one another, and make a few plans for the property in Texas.

CHAPTER SEVEN

-

One of the things Pru learned about Sven that winter was he was the inveterate planner, from a long time past. Sven was on the radio almost every day that winter, cultivating existing contacts, and making more. He was going to need at least some help to do what he and Pru had decided to do with the land in Texas, based on Sven's planning from long before the attack.

The basic overall plan was to do what Sven had planned to do after retirement, for something to do to keep him busy. He'd been buying things while he had the good paying jobs, planning for his retirement and for what had come.

The first part of the plan was to recover and assemble his prefab retirement home. A custom manufactured log home and out buildings he'd bought and paid for while working in Montana on a road project that was near a prefab log home manufacturer. Everything for the off grid home complex was loaded on four flat beds and in two box/reefer semi-trailers stored at one of his friends' place near Tulsa. That friend was one of those that had died at his brother's house.

Sven made arrangements to get six former independent truckers in the Tulsa area with their own trucks that were running to pick up the trailers and take them to Hondo. Sven and Pru would meet them at their homes and provide fuel for the trucks for the trip.

Sven and Pru set out as soon as they thought the worst of the winter weather was over. They made a direct run to Tulsa, being very careful. They had no trouble at all, seeing very few people. The second post at-tack winter had been as bad as the first. It had finished many of those that had eked out an existence after the attack and the first winter.

Sven stopped at each of the truckers' homes, three of which were staying together in a ranch house not too far from Jack's place, putting enough of the treated diesel from the Suburban's custom trailer tank to get them to Jack's. Sven told them there would be more there. He saw the doubt in all three of the men's faces.

In convoy, the group stopped at the gate of the wrecking yard that had been Jack's livelihood. He'd had a decent business salvaging parts from wrecked cars to repair other wrecked vehicles. There was a section in the yard where thirty or so semi-trailers were all lined up, some stripped down to almost nothing. Others still complete.

The ones Sven was interested in were some of the complete ones. Much to the drivers' amazement, Sven pointed out the trailers he wanted them to take to Texas.

"Those old junkers?" asked one of the three drivers that lived not too far away. "They're here for scrap. Liable to fall apart on the way!"

"Not these," Sven replied. "Take a look at the tires, kingpins, and running gear."

The drivers took Sven at his word and did a thorough inspection of all the trailers Sven indicated. One of the drivers walked over to the Suburban where Sven and Pru were waiting, and said "Okay. Except for some tires with some weather checking, and being low, those all look like they'll make the trip."

Sven looked at the other drivers as they walked up. It was a consensus. Then, again to their surprise, Sven took a portable fuel pump from one of the toolboxes of the Suburban's trailer, got up on a seven-thousand-gallon tank trailer and lowered it into a hatch, after unlocking the weather resistant combination lock.

"You telling me you got fuel in that truck?" yelled up the man that had called the trailers junkers.

Sven smiled down at them as Pru started the generator on the trailer and plugged in the pump. "Probably a good thing you guys didn't know, huh?"

There was some good-natured joking that Sven was right. Had they known, the fuel probably wouldn't still be there.

Sven filled the trucks' diesel tanks in turn, giving them full loads of fuel. "It's all treated with PRI-D," Sven told them when there was some suggestion that it might not be good fuel.

The trucks all fueled, and the pump put away, Sven and Pru stayed out of the way as the truckers got the trailers all connected, tires aired up, and air pressure built up to test the trailer brakes. When all seemed in order, Sven let the convoy out of the salvage yard and closed the gates behind them.

After a check run of a couple of miles, Sven led the convoy away from Tulsa and toward Hondo, Texas. It was some convoy, especially for the day. There were six semi-trucks of various makes, pulling two trailers each. There were a total of four loaded flatbeds, two loaded box/reefers, two loaded tank trailers, one empty tanker, and three empty box/reefers. The Suburban was pulling its custom tandem wheel support trailer and the last two toy haulers with all the remaining toys.

It took a week to get to the property, and a day to get the trailers set where Sven wanted them on the property. Sven paid off four of the drivers, and they left, with full fuel tanks again, a month's worth of food for four, each, and a bit of gold and silver, traveling paired up in two of the trucks. Sven had managed to buy two of the trucks.

The other two drivers were also paid, but Sven had made arrangements with them to stay and do some additional work locally. That work included bringing several pieces of construction equipment to the property from where they were scattered here and there in the area. Sven bought a few of them, but most were clearly abandoned, and he took them without compunction.

The local work done, and without the toy haulers, Sven led the way back to Oklahoma to pick up four more empty trailers—a flatbed, an equipment trailer, and two box/reefers. The box/reefers were filled from the various caches Sven had around the retreat and at Jack's.

The flatbed and most of the equipment trailer were loaded up with all the healthy fruit and nut trees and any grape vines they could find that weren't tied down, so to speak. They found them mostly from nurseries along the route, but some from Jack's place, and from a couple of abandoned orchards. A Bobcat A300 utility loader with a tree spade did the digging and placing the trees on the trailers, and then rode the tail end of the equipment trailer when on the road.

After paying off the drivers for the additional work, Sven and Pru, with Traven's help on Sundays, began putting in long hours getting the trees and grape vines planted, and large areas of berry patches put in. A solar pump with solar panel did simple duty to irrigate the plantings and pro-vide water for the tent camp Pru and Sven were living in on the property.

Following the plans of the prefab log house, Sven used a backhoe he'd found to dig the basement, and ready the garage and parking pads, and a length of driveway. A second basement was dug, for the detached work-shop, and a hole for a swimming pool, with pad for pool house. Another area was prepped for a concrete floored pole barn to go in. There were two more building footings and floors prepared for smaller buildings. Plastic sheet and rebar were put down. July 4th was two weeks away.

It took a week working at the abandoned concrete plant to get four concrete trucks running, and everything set up to start mixing, moving, and pouring concrete. He hired several locals that knew a thing or two about concrete and with their help the basement floors, the pool, and the pads were poured and finished.

While waiting for the concrete to cure enough to form the basement walls, Sven and Pru were unloading the flatbed trailers and getting everything ready for a house raising. Finally, they were able to start the forming of the basement walls. It took a hard week to get them done. The small crew Sven had put together earlier was eager for more of the food paying work and helped pour the basement walls.

Another wait for the concrete basement walls to cure found Sven and Pru in the process of putting in the septic system for the house and out-buildings. Sven had most of the materials needed in with the package, although they had to find some additional items, but had no problem doing so.

Sven and Pru hosted a big barbeque on the property for everyone willing to help raise the major portions of the house and shop. He and Pru provided foods from Sven's stores that people had been without since the attack, in addition to a roast pig and half a beef they bought from Big Ben for the event.

It took two and a half days to get the work done. Sven sent the remains of the barbeque home with all those that had helped, plus a little bit of silver coin each, in appreciation. One man in particular had impressed Sven with his hard, expert work and Sven asked him to work on a regular basis.

"Sure 'ting, Boss. Just tell me when you need me, and I'll be here."

"Well, Harlen, tomorrow for sure. We'll just have to decide on a day to day basis, but I'll guarantee you at least a month's food each month, until winter, no matter how much you work."

"Fine wit' me, Boss. I'll be here first light." Harlen got on his old Harley-Davidson motorcycle and took off, the throaty rumble of the Harley shaking the ground slightly.

It took the rest of the summer to finish the house and shop, but when it was done, the place was a sight to behold. The place was totally off the now non-existent grid, but had all the necessities, plus a few luxuries.

Elaine took Pru aside after visiting for the first time since the house had been half completed. "Pru! This place is wonderful! Would it be…would it be okay if I got married here?"

Pru hugged Elaine. "So, he asked, huh?"

"Just last week. There's a traveling preacher now and we can have a real service."

"Of course, you can get married here!"

After Elaine and Pru told Sven he insisted on it.

Two weeks before Thanksgiving Elaine married Ben at the new house and the two moved into one of the several houses on the ranch property as husband and wife. Traven, grown amazingly over the past year, had given the bride away, and Pru had been Maid of Honor. The reception was at the Ranch. Again Sven and Pru provided some foods from Sven's storage that were nearly impossible to get now.

It was only several weeks later that everyone found out that Pru and Sven had gone before the preacher and said their vows, with only Traven and Harlen present as witnesses. They hadn't wanted to take anything away from Elaine's wedding, but wanted to tie the knot while the preacher was there on his last visit for the summer.

With the alternative Sven and Pru offered Traven, Traven moved to the property. Working quickly Traven helped put in a pole corral for his two horses, and move a small prefab yard barn from an abandoned property nearby. The little barn would be a stop gap measure until Traven could make arrangements to build a larger barn on the property for his intended business of horse breeder and trainer.

With two loads of hay on trailers, and a tarped load of corn on another flatbed with short sideboards added, the feed for the horses was taken care of for the winter. Traven and Harlen helped Sven get the shop set up the way he wanted.

Sven went over to see Big Ben to let him know about his new business.

"Doing what? You're a cat skinner you said. I don't need a cat skinner."

"Well, you see, I grew up around heavy equipment, and became a professional after I got out of the Navy. In the Navy, I became a machinist. When I was in high school a friend of my dad was an old time blacksmith and he taught me some things when I asked him to help me make a knife out of a file. So I can do blacksmith work and machining with the equipment at my shop. I worked on a house construction crew while I was going to college, got the tools and such for carpentry. Fix up just about anything fixable, if I do say so myself. I can also grind wheat into flour on a small scale. Make soap. Sharpen knives as well as making them. Few other things, and more to come as I expand."

"I see. Well... Hum... If I have anything needs fixing I might just call you on the radio."

"That's all I ask, Ben. Thanks."

Big Ben watched Sven go back to the Suburban, shaking his head. "Was purely wrong about that family," he told Melinda when he went inside. "That Elaine is going to be a good one for Ben. And Traven...he's going to be competition one of these days. He's got a knack for horses and works as much as most men."

Sven made the rounds in the area, including going into San Antonio to advertise his repair business, and Pru's sewing service. He would wait to announce some of his other offerings until they were ready.

Harlen moved his old trailer to the property and hooked up to Sven's solar electrical system. It was easier for him to live there than travel back and forth even the short distance away he lived every day.

Sven, Harlen, Traven, and Pru continued building projects as fall came and went, with winter right behind. The large icehouse was ready when the weather turned. Sven, Harlen, and Traven filled all the rubber ice block molds Sven had each night to freeze, and then stored the blocks of ice in the icehouse the following morning. By spring the icehouse was full to the gills with precious ice.

Pru was pregnant and unable to do any labor, except for her sewing. Sven and Traven took care of everything else.

As soon as they could that spring the large commercial greenhouse was installed on the foundation laid the previous summer and a greenhouse garden started, using non-hybrid seeds. Sven had ordered the greenhouse with some special features.

There was room on the southern end for several rabbit hutches built over raised worm beds. The rabbits' droppings would provide the food needed by the worms. Fish tanks were partially buried under the worm beds so the fish could be fed easily. The arrangement gave much additional protein to the group, with enough to trade once the operation reached full scale.

A much smaller, but similar greenhouse was erected over the swimming pool. An outside garden was tilled and planted with more of the non-hybrid seeds Sven had stored in abundance. A chicken tractor was build and Sven obtained a rooster and several hens.

Sven had kept his eye on a large pole barn in the area. The owner had been reluctant to sell it, but that spring Sven contacted him again. The man was more than willing to let the building go for a generous payment of food. The man and his family had nearly starved that winter.

Two weeks after the deal was cut, the building was torn down and re-erected on Sven and Pru's property. They didn't even lose any height, as the poles of the barn were actually treated 8 x 8's, sitting on galvanized brackets in the foundation. Sven made identical brackets and installed them in his foundation. It wasn't sheer luck that the building fit the foundation. Sven had designed it that way with that exact pole barn in mind.

With Pru due any day, Elaine came over to the property to stay with her and help with the chores. Sven made arrangements for a doctor to come out and stay for a few days, to be there when Pru gave birth.

Everything was ready, with the doctor in a travel trailer Sven had acquired for the purpose. Pru had good timing. The doctor from San Antonio had been there only a day and a half when she went into labor.

Fortunately, Sven had everything needed, as the doctor had run out of supplies the first winter. There was only one small problem and the doctor was able to deal with it with no consequences and the next thing they knew, Sven and Pru were the proud parents of a healthy son, Shawn.

Sven took the doctor home two days later and ensured that he was well paid. Elaine stayed another two weeks to help Pru with any number of things, as she needed to take it easy for at least that long.

Sven got a major job a few days later. A local farmer needed a cultivator completely rebuilt. It was the first of many such jobs as equipment started to break or wear out. It wasn't like they were making it new anymore, and parts were harder and harder to come by.

By fall the rabbits and fish were producing enough to begin selling a few. The chickens were also laying quite a few healthy eggs, with a few brooding hens taking care of chicks.

And the greenhouse was going great guns. The outside garden produced enough to be preserved by the family for future use. The fruit, nut, and grape orchards were taking hold. They lost less than fifteen percent of the trees they had transplanted. It would be another year before there was any major production.

The ice had not moved as well as Sven thought it would. But he didn't give up and filled two of the box/reefers with ice when the icehouse filled early in the winter. It was another harsh winter, the worse so far since the attack. There was snow at the property up to four feet deep at times. From the radio reports he was getting, and those regular contacts missing, Sven wondered just how bad it was getting in the northern latitudes.

A contact in eastern Nevada informed Sven the Ruby Mountains near him had not been snow free since the first winter. The snow was estimated to be forty feet deep at the melt line. No one would venture a guess how deep it was higher.

A couple of people around Branson indicated they were at seven feet of snow accumulation by Christmas and still growing.

Sven, Traven, Pru, with Shawn in her arms, were sitting in the nice warm living room in early March the next spring. "I don't think we would have made it, even with your prior planning, further north," Pru told Sven.

"Good planning," Traven said, smiling. He was seventeen now, a man in all ways. His skill with horses was extraordinary, and he was busy the summer months breaking the many horses being raised in the area, when he wasn't helping Sven. Besides the colt and filly he'd taken in the first trade, he had one more owed him by Big Ben for working the horses at his ranch, and four more from other people for whom he'd provided the same service the previous year. The only thing holding him back was a good barn to shelter them during the winter.

He and Sven had been working on that and a barn would be raised that spring, barring any major trouble. It would be the used portions of several barns in the area that were in various states of decay. Only the best materials out of each of them would be used to get what Traven wanted. Three of the farms from which the barn parts were coming had grain silos. Those silos would be moved and erected, too.

When the work was done, and the horses that had been promised to Traven delivered afterward the next spring, Traven had a small, but full-scale horse raising operation going. It would be three years before he had any to sell, but that time would come and Traven's vision was finally coming to fruition.

With a going business, a secure place to live, the means and willingness to defend it, and some jingling money in his pocket, being almost twenty-one, six feet two inches tall, long brown hair, and dancing brown eyes, it was a tossup which of the available young ladies in that part of Texas would wind up marrying him.

When Sven took him aside one day and asked him about his future he replied, "I've got a plan, Sven. Planning pays off, you know." Both men laughed.

THE END

THANK YOU FOR READING
"PLANNING PAYS OFF"
By
Jerry D. Young

LIKE THIS BOOK?

See more great books at
www.creativetexts.com

"SIMPLER TIMES"
"BUGGING HOME"
"THE SLOW ROAD"
"LOW PROFILE"
"RUDY'S PREPAREDNESS SHOP"
"CME: CORONAL MASS EJECTION"
"HOME SWEET BUNKER"
"THE HERMIT"

& MANY MORE GREAT
POST-APOCALYPTIC FICTION
& OTHER TITLES

THANK YOU!

MEET THE AUTHOR

Jerry D Young was born at home, in Senath, Missouri July 3, 1953. At age 5 the family rented a small farm house on an active farm, 40 miles southwest of St. Louis. While the family weren't farmers, they lived something of a homestead type life, raising a milk cow, sometimes two, and calves, a pig or two, chickens, and the occasional goat. Along with the stock, a large garden helped to feed Jerry's three brothers and two sisters for several years. Fishing and hunting contributed to the pantry, as did foraging the wild edibles on the property.

At the age of 14, the family, minus a brother and two sisters that were now adults and on their own, moved back to Senath. Having been encouraged from an early age to read, Jerry was a regular patron of the Senath Branch Library. A love of a good story was born within him, and shortly before graduating high school, for a lack of stories that he liked at the library, he began to write short vignettes, and started taking notes for stories that he wanted to tell. Jerry eventually began to write in earnest and now has more than 100 titles to his credit.

www.ingramcontent.com/pod-product-compliance
Lightning Source LLC
Chambersburg PA
CBHW020639110726
47899CB00002B/822